Falling for the Cat Guy

by

Kate Berberich

Carson Mills, Book One

Cover Art by *Kristian Norris*

The Wild Rose Press, Inc.
PO Box 708
Adams Basin, NY 14410-0708
Visit us at www.thewildrosepress.com

Publishing History
First Edition, 2024
Trade Paperback ISBN 978-1-5092-5767-6
Digital ISBN 978-1-5092-5768-3

Carson Mills, Book One
Published in the United States of America

Dedication

This one's for Brian and Lisa and all the other real-life heroes who make a difference every day, one tiny life at a time.

Chapter One

"Jeez, Maggie...are you sure about this place? This looks like the kitchen at my grandma's house."

Maggie Edwards set down the bulky box containing her microwave and stretched her aching back. "Well, since they converted this place into apartments in the sixties, it probably is the same as your grandma's." She glanced around the cozy space. The bright-flowered wallpaper begged for a quaint wall clock—maybe something from one of those public television catalogs? Or— "Are there any antique shops around here?"

"Do I look like I know anything about antique shops?" Ted Ambrose opened one of the polished wooden cabinets, no doubt looking for snacks. "Aren't these kinda small?"

"Nope, they're just the right size. When do I have time to cook? This place is cute, and someone put a lot of work into it. Besides, all I need is for the fuses not to blow when I use the microwave or coffee pot." She opened the retro poppy-red fridge—whatever the vintage, it worked. The interior was nice and cool—and the landlord had left a six-pack of bottled water. She tossed one to her long-time partner, fellow paramedic, and substitute big brother, who caught the bottle, unscrewed the cap, and guzzled half in one go.

He wiped his mouth with the back of his hand. "But your old place was great."

She selected a bottle, opened it, and took a long drink, then replaced the cap. *Let's not spill things before I even finish moving in.* "Yeah, except that place was never mine, it was always Jack's, and he's welcome to it. Now he's free to go find himself a pretty face who has no ambition beyond hanging on his arm at parties and—"

"And backing his precious career." Ted slung an affectionate arm around her in a rough hug. "Guy's a jerk, and he didn't deserve you. It's still a sweet condo."

She allowed herself a moment's comfort from her colleague, then sucked in a deep breath. "Jack's complex had lots of activity happening when I needed to sleep. This is more convenient to work. Carson Mills is off the beaten path. The street's peaceful and quiet—"

As if on cue, a dog started barking right outside. Loudly.

"You were saying?" Ted snickered. As usual, his sandy hair stuck up in all directions, and his shirt looked like he'd slept in it. Despite his somewhat less-than-professional demeanor, he had the steadiest hands of anyone she'd ever worked with, and an indispensable knack for setting people at ease.

"This is mine." She grabbed her notes for placing the furniture she'd retrieved from storage.

Outside, the dog kept barking, accompanied by the dulcet tones of several off-duty firefighters.

"Shoo!"

"Somebody grab that mutt."

"You grab him."

Maggie picked her way through the maze of boxes to the bay window and looked outside. A very large, very handsome, and utterly untrained dalmatian lunged at the guys unloading her belongings from the rental truck.

The dog barked again, jumping wildly at her friends. She sighed and headed for the stairs.

****

Brad MacKenzie glared at his computer screen. Did this guy not read the specs at all? This book was intended for nine-and ten-year-olds, not high school students. *I'll have to revise the whole thing to bring the vocabulary down to the correct reading level. And what's Cuthbert barking his fool head off about now?*

He reached for a cookie, groping around a bit when he didn't find one. A small fluffy calico ball of mischief took advantage of his inattention to hop on his lap and snatch a pad of sticky notes with one white paw. "Nixie, get down."

Nixie did not.

"Hollyn, call Nixie, will you?"

Hollyn's snort was clearly audible from the front entry. "Yeah, 'cuz she's so obedient."

"Shake a packet of treats or something. I'm trying to work."

"And I'm not?"

"Well, since you're here and not at your own clinic, I don't know what you're doing." He set Nixie on the floor and fumbled for a cookie, again encountering empty tabletop. He finally turned his head and frowned. No cookies. Hadn't Elsie put a plate there when she arrived? Wait—when was that? He saved his document and stood, stretching and wandering toward the front hall. He nudged a couple of jingle balls out of the way with his toe and stooped to grab a pen one of the cats absconded with.

His sister looked up from her laptop. "Oh,

good…you're not dead."

He and Se were sound asleep on their favorite perches on the big cat tree. They didn't even stir at Brad's approach.

"Didn't Elsie bring cookies?"

"She did. You grunted something about formatting without looking up from your screen." Hollyn flicked her braid of long brown hair over her shoulder and wriggled her nose to settle her glasses. "Someone's moving into the middle apartment in the old Adams place, and Elsie thought they might appreciate snacks."

"I'm on a deadline. That's how we keep the lights on." He paused. "And I appreciate snacks. And Elsie."

"Then you should learn to say thank you when she brings you stuff. Jeez, I wish Cuthbert would shut up."

"Nice attitude from a vet."

"He's not my patient. I'd have advised training him a long time ago if he was. As it is, he's a menace."

"And Elsie's out there with food?" A sudden jolt of adrenaline buzzed through his veins. "I'm gonna go make sure she's okay."

He shoved his feet into shoes—after dumping a plastic spring toy out of one—and caught Nixie before she could dash out the door. "Take her, will you?"

Hollyn rolled her eyes but cuddled the wayward mischief maker.

Brad pulled the door shut and strode across the street. It was late enough Saturday morning that neighbors were out and about, taking advantage of the unseasonably warm first weekend of October to pack up their summer lawn furniture or get a jump on Halloween. The breeze carried a hint of charcoal smoke from someone's backyard grill. The Rogers family across the street industriously unwound and inspected a prodigious number of extension cords and light strings. That might have been alarming, if not for the van with "licensed electrician" painted on the side parked in the driveway.

Carson Circle contained a hodge-podge of rambling old Victorian houses. Each home reflected both its own faded glory and its current owner's personality. Some yards featured flower or vegetable gardens. Others sported intricate paint jobs, like the famed painted ladies of San Francisco, with matching dog houses and detached garages. Yard signs and library boxes dotted the neighborhood, not to mention campaign signs for both local and statewide elections. *Home sweet home*.

Like a couple of the other larger homes, a new owner had divided the Adams house into apartments. The olive green clapboard siding and rusty red trim were a season or so overdue for a coat of fresh paint, but the property was homey and welcoming. Two gnarled apple trees grew in the front yard. Fallen leaves and fruit littered the ground beneath them.

A rental truck sat in front and several guys unloaded while fending off an enthusiastic dalmatian. A tall fellow in a county fire department T-shirt shielded Elsie and held her plate of cookies up out of Cuthbert's determined reach.

"Hey, pal—is this your dog?"

"Hell, no," Brad replied, lunging for Cuthbert's collar. "If he was mine, he'd be secured in his own yard—and he'd have gone to obedience school. Down, Cuthbert." *It would be so nice if someone besides me ever tried to control him.*

A craggy-faced old man with grizzly gray hair emerged from the immaculate yard of the enormous old mansion at the far end of the cul-de-sac. He hobbled forward at an impressive pace, considering he leaned on a cane. "Unhand my dog, MacKenzie."

"Shh, it's okay, buddy." Brad turned his attention to Cuthbert's owner. "We've talked about this, Mr. Carson. This wouldn't be an issue if you kept Cuthbert in your own yard. He was running loose and jumping at these people."

"Well, they're causing a commotion, aren't they? Maybe even a fire hazard. Maybe I'll call the fire department. What do you think of that?"

A woman with sugar-brown curls pulled back in a messy bun, and a pretty heart-shaped face clambered down the porch steps. She had green eyes.

Cat's eyes.

"Sir, we are the fire department. We're not blocking any hydrants or obstructing the flow of traffic. I assure you, if our colleagues needed to get in here, we'd move the truck immediately."

The old man looked her up and down and harrumphed derisively. "A little thing like you is a fireman?"

"Maggie's the best paramedic in the county," one of the guys informed him. "And there might just come a day when you're glad to have her for a neighbor. Now, could you please restrain your dog? There are ordinances, you know. He jumped at this lady."

"And there're no tags on his collar," Ted added.

Mr. Carson wrestled Cuthbert's collar from Brad's grasp and perambulated toward his own house. He paused along the way to glare at a little girl playing hopscotch on the sidewalk.

Not-so-polite mutterings followed the old man's

departure.

"Some neighborhood you picked, Maggie," Ted quipped.

She ignored him, going to check on Elsie. "I'm Maggie Edwards. I'm a paramedic. Are you okay, ma'am?"

"I'm fine, dear." Elsie peeked around the tall firefighter who'd protected her from Cuthbert. "Your friend kept Cuthbert from clobbering me."

"I'm not sure who's the bigger menace—the dog or the owner," Maggie replied.

"Oh, it's not Cuthbert's fault." Elsie told her. "Dalmatians need to run and play. He'd be better off on a farm with a couple of teenage boys."

"And a trip to obedience school," Brad added.

Maggie turned to him and extended her hand. "Thanks for your help. I'm Maggie."

"I'm Brad. Brad MacKenzie. Um…welcome to the neighborhood?"

She laughed and shook his hand. Small, warm fingers closed around his in a firm grip. He held on a few seconds longer than he probably should have.

"Yeah, that was quite the welcome, all right. You were great with that dog."

Brad scrubbed a hand through his hair. *Why are people so much harder to talk to than animals? Especially smart, pretty people with kind eyes and beautiful smiles who are surrounded by guys who make their living running into burning buildings. Heroes. I'm just a guy who rescues cats.*

And his new neighbor stood there waiting for a response.

"Well, I'm better with cats, but like Elsie said,

Cuthbert's not a bad dog, really, he's just hopelessly untrained."

A couple more loud barks echoed down the street and behind them someone in the Adams house slammed a window shut.

Maggie turned and glanced up at the third floor, frowning. Brad rolled his eyes at the edge of the curtain caught in the window frame.

"That's your upstairs neighbor, Butch," Elsie explained. "He's the night watchman at the old paint factory."

"Hey, Mags—you wanna show us where the rest of this stuff goes?"

Maggie raised an eyebrow. "You sure figured out where the cookies go." The pumpkin-shaped plate in Elsie's hands was empty except for a scattering of crumbs.

"Plenty more where those came from. I'm Elsie Tatum, by the way. I volunteer at The Clowder."

"The Clowder?"

"A clowder is a group of kittens," Elsie explained.

"The house across the street, with the cat flag." Brad nodded toward the butter-yellow house enclosed by a neat white picket fence. "I run a cat rescue—"

"Wait—haven't I seen you on the local news? You're the Cat Guy."

Brad smiled modestly—he hoped. "My sister and I do pet safety segments on the local cable channel for the Carson Mills Cares campaign."

"Hey, Maggie," Ted bellowed out the window.

"Coming." She turned to Brad and Elsie. "The natives are getting restless."

"Can I give you a hand?" Brad offered.

"I thought you had a deadline?" Elsie reminded him.

"I…" Brad's cheeks warmed. Fifteen years out of Elsie's English lit classroom and she still had that effect on him.

"It's fine, really." Maggie chuckled—a warm, pleasant sound he wouldn't mind hearing more of. "There's barely room to move up there as it is."

"Would you like help organizing your kitchen, dear? You can't trust a man to get that sort of thing right."

Maggie winked at her. "Maybe in a day or so? Let's let these guys do the heavy lifting."

"Well, if you need a break, come on over and meet the kittens." She elbowed Brad none too subtly.

"Um, yeah. Please come on over any time."

Chapter Two

Monday morning, Maggie visited the butter-yellow house across the street. The MacKenzie house was one of the smaller homes on the circle, just two stories and an attic clad with pale gray shingles, plus a matching detached garage. The wooden sign on the white picket fence read "The Clowder." Orange and yellow leaves scattered the lawn and crunched underfoot. A library case full of books with cat titles stood at the end of the driveway, and a couple of large planters labeled "catnip" flanked the porch steps.

Chubby kittens in ghost and witch costumes frolicked on a purple flag, snapping in the breeze, and a doormat decorated with cats in witch hats welcomed guests. Two gray tabby cats snoozed blissfully on a large cat tree inside the front window.

Elsie Tatum, the sweet-faced older lady who'd been so generous with cookies, cupcakes, and other goodies answered the door. A headband adorned with sparkly black cat ears held back her faded blonde hair. She carried a roll of paper towels, a bottle of spray cleaner, and a squirming calico cat tucked under her arm.

Maggie darted inside, and Elsie shut the door just as the kitty wriggled loose. She put her paws on Maggie's leg and sniffed ecstatically.

"Get down," Elsie scolded.

"Good morning, Ms. Tatum." Maggie covered her

mouth and swallowed a yawn.

"Call me Elsie. Nixie, get down." She nudged the cat gently with her foot. "How's the unpacking coming?"

Maggie shrugged. "It's…coming. There's a path, anyway."

"Goodness, you look tired, dear. Would you like to sit and have a coffee? And maybe a cinnamon bun or two?"

"That sounds wonderful, Ms.—Elsie—but I was wondering if Brad was available?"

Elsie raised an eyebrow and smiled. "He and Hollyn are settling a couple of kittens they trapped this morning. I'm not sure how far into the intake they are. They never let me handle them until they've been tested and vaccinated. Is there anything I can do?"

"I don't think so." Maggie stifled another yawn. *I want out of this uniform. A hot bath, the drapes pulled shut, my flannel pjs…I know where those are, right? And Butch's car is gone, so I don't have to worry about him tromping up and down the stairs waking me up.*

"I really think you should come in and sit, dear."

Footsteps thundered from somewhere inside the house.

"Elsie, did I hear the doorbell?" Brad called. "Is the delivery here?"

"Yes, you did. Mind the—"

"Dammit!"

"I was just going to clean that up."

Maggie blinked. Her handsome neighbor hobbled to the door with one sock foot and the other bare. His brown hair was a bit scruffy—not unkempt, exactly, more like he had more important things to do than fuss in front of a mirror. *A refreshing change from—nope—not gonna think about him. Nuts, I'm woolgathering.* She roused herself from her comfy slouch against his doorframe.

"Um…hi. I just came off shift, and there's a delivery on my front porch that belongs to you. A big one."

Brad leaned against the wall, balanced on one foot. "I'm expecting a shipment of supplies—mostly food and litter."

"Lots of big boxes? I would have brought it over, but I think you'll need a hand truck or something."

"No worries—we have one. I'm really sorry about this. Our regular delivery guy must be off today. Give me and Hollyn about five minutes to clean up, and we'll move the cartons."

"I can help, too," Elsie insisted.

Brad smiled and brushed a kiss to her forehead. "I need you to moderate the chat room."

"I'm not made of glass, you know."

"I do know, but chat can get out of hand pretty quickly if someone doesn't keep an eye on things." Brad winked at Maggie over Elsie's head.

"Well, there is a lot of chatter about Community Day right now."

"Don't remind me."

"What's Community Day?" Maggie asked.

"A couple of years ago the town council voted to replace Columbus Day with Community Day," Elsie explained. "There's a parade and a craft fair—"

"Wait—is that the blood drive I'm working?" Maggie shook her head, willing away the cobwebs.

"Yes, dear. And local nonprofits have tents. Including The Clowder." She said the last with a significant look in Brad's direction.

"You and Hollyn—"

12

"You are the face of this organization, Brad." Elsie crossed her arms and stared up at him. "So you're going to wear a decent shirt and smile and have your picture taken with the mayor."

Maggie pressed her lips together to contain a small huff of laughter. Elsie pivoted to her.

"And you are going to get some rest before you fall down."

Maggie made an effort to straighten and look alert. "I should have grabbed at least one box and brought it with me. That was stupid."

"It's not your problem." Brad paused and took a good look at her. "Just how long are those shifts of yours?"

"You've just stumbled on one of the great mysteries of the universe. Last night was supposed to be a standard eight hours, but there was a bad accident on the highway. We had to airlift the driver to the medical center. Then we had to contact the family to pick up a toddler who was also in the car. There wasn't a social worker available, and the child attached herself to me..."

"So you were up all night looking after someone else's little kid? After responding to a major accident?"

"Something like that."

"You come with me, dear." Elsie tugged on her arm. "I'm going to feed you some breakfast while Brad and Hollyn move those boxes."

"Oh, it's really not—"

"Don't even bother arguing. Elsie used to be a schoolteacher, and I guarantee she'll win."

****

Brad hobbled down the basement steps, flinching each time his bare foot hit the rough boards.

"I need you to come give me a hand."

"Are the supplies here?" Hollyn kept her voice low so as not to disturb the two half-grown kittens she'd finally gotten settled. She pulled the door shut behind her with a soft click.

"In a manner of speaking. They're on the porch of the Adams place." He pulled off his remaining sock and fired it into the washing machine.

She fished a small light out of her pocket and set it on the counter. "No sign of ringworm with the blacklight." She glanced at his feet. "What happened to the other one?"

"Hairball, right at the top of the steps."

She snickered and unzipped the rustling white coverall she wore over her clothes. "So, two dozen cases of cat food were delivered across the street to the house with the Pride flag instead of the house with the cat flag?" She shook her head. "Unbelievable."

"Yup. Plus, the litter." Brad deposited his discarded coverall in the washing machine, along with towels from the top of the overflowing hamper. He held out his hand for his sister's, shifting his weight from one foot to the other on the chilled tile floor.

"And you know this how?" She peeled off the suit and chucked it to her brother.

He caught the coverall and added it to the machine, along with a generous dose of detergent and sanitizer. "Maggie came to tell us."

"Did she, now?"

Brad looked over his shoulder as he scrubbed his hands at the slop sink. "She did and stop smirking."

"Who's smirking?"

"Stop—whatever you're thinking, just stop." He

stepped aside so she could have a turn at the sink.

"What? Elsie says she's nice. And pretty."

"So what if she is?"

"Single, as far as I can tell," Hollyn continued. "Look, Brad…you're not the school book nerd anymore. You're a published author and respected animal rescuer—both of which would look great on a dating profile. Except you don't need a dating profile because an amazing single woman just moved in across the street."

"Will you shut up?" Brad hissed as they headed to the stairs.

"Is she still here?"

"She is. She had a rough night at work, and Elsie's feeding her."

Hollyn smirked and clattered up the stairs ahead of her sibling. "Hi, Maggie. I'm Brad's sister, Hollyn."

"Hi…you're the vet, right?" Maggie pushed back her stool.

"Sit," Elsie ordered without turning from whatever she was stirring in the skillet.

"I'd listen to her if I were you," Brad advised. "We'll retrieve our supplies from your porch before your neighbors complain."

"I should really—"

"Sit there and eat." Hollyn stretched a hand toward the skillet.

Elsie slapped the hand away absently and continued cooking.

****

"This is why I sprang for the convertible hand truck." Brad stacked another carton on the flatbed.

"Yeah, yeah." Hollyn followed behind him with

another. "Still doesn't help with steps."

"But it beats carrying each separate box across the street."

One of Carson Mills' two police cars rolled to a silent stop at the curb, interrupting their cheerful wrangling. An officer with leathery dark skin and wise brown eyes climbed out, settling a worn "Smokey Bear" hat on his head. "Hey, Doc MacKenzie, Mr. MacKenzie."

"Chief Parker," Hollyn acknowledged.

"I received a call about a possible porch piracy in progress. Know anything about that?"

Hollyn rolled her eyes. "Seriously?"

Brad's lips thinned, and he scrubbed a hand over his face.

"I know. The individual is notorious for filing questionable complaints, but I must investigate anything filed through official channels. The one time I decide to brush him off will be a legitimate call, and I'll have a retailer breathing down my neck about having to replace stolen goods."

"Our neighbor came home from work and saw these had been delivered here by mistake." Brad set his driver's license next to the label on one of the boxes.

"That's fine, Mr. MacKenzie." Chief Parker snapped a perfunctory photo with his phone. "Oh—hey there, Maggie."

"Hi, Chief." She climbed the steps to her new front porch and drooped against the railing. "How's the arm?"

"Right as rain, thanks." He pivoted to include the MacKenzie siblings in the conversation. "The surgeon said if I hadn't received such great care on the scene, I might have lost mobility."

16

Maggie blushed under his praise. "Is there a problem here?" She glanced from the officer to her erstwhile neighbors.

"Mr. Carson called in a possible robbery. Had to make an official appearance."

"The old guy with the dog? What's his problem, anyway?"

Chief Parker pushed his hat back on his head. "Well, he's the last of the Carsons."

"What—you mean—" Maggie gestured at the street sign.

"Yup. Carson, as in Carson Circle, where we're standing. Also, the town of Carson Mills and the mills themselves. He's the last of 'em. The mills went bust when he was a kid. He never got over the fact his family don't run this town anymore."

"He certainly seems to think he runs this street," Maggie observed.

"He's a bitter old man with nothing to live for but his dog." The chief nodded toward the end of the circle at the turreted mansion brooding over the neighborhood.

"That, and complaining about other people's yards," Brad observed with a sour grimace.

"And kids, and cars," Hollyn chimed in.

Maggie glanced at the property at the end of the circle. The house could be pretty with some window boxes or colorful shutters. Instead, it reminded her of a paint ad—Boringest Beige, maybe? Coffee colored shingles covered the roof and turrets, and gloomy drapes shrouded the windows. A precisely trimmed lawn encircled the property. No flowers or decorations broke up the emptiness of the yard. Not even any campaign signs for the hotly contested upcoming gubernatorial race, even though the rest of the circle was peppered with them. And no fence to contain a large and active dog. "How long has he been alone in that big old place?"

"Save your sympathy," Hollyn snorted.

"Now, Doc—" the chief began.

"No. If he was even remotely civil, I might feel sorry for him, but all he does is make trouble for everyone who lives here. He's been that way since me and Brad were kids."

"He does seem to think he's a one-man homeowner's association. Which reminds me—he's been complaining about the leaves again. Like I got nothing better to do." His phone chirped and he glanced at the screen, then tucked it away. "Anyway, I'll be on my way, seeing as there's no actual porch piracy occurring here."

"Chief Parker!" A neighbor with red hair and the temper to match stomped out of his yard, heading their way. "Did that old coot call you? He's been yelling at my little girl again."

"Now calm down, Nate. Which exact old coot are you talking about?"

Nate jerked his chin toward the end of the circle. "You know exactly who I mean."

The chief cleared his throat, meaningfully.

"Pardon me, folks." Nate's face twisted in an obvious attempt to control his temper—which didn't quite succeed. "Look, I paid five grand for that sidewalk. It's in front of my house, where I can see my kid from the window. She's playing with chalk, for crying out loud. It washes away in the rain. She's not 'defacing' anything."

Chief Parker raised his hand. "No, of course she's

not. I've told him repeatedly to stop abusing the system. The only way I get involved in something like that is if someone was writing cuss words or such, which I know your daughter wouldn't do." His phone chirped again. "Now, since we've determined you aren't stealing anything," he glanced at Brad, "and your daughter isn't defacing anything," he looked at Nate, "I need to go put the fear of God into a bunch of high school boys who are trying to buy beer. Nate, why don't you help Doc MacKenzie with those boxes?"

"Of course, Chief." Nate nodded to Maggie, then took over loading the flatbed from Hollyn.

"Give my regards to Elsie, would you?"

"Sure thing, Chief." Brad waved as the chief got into his car and pulled away.

Maggie straightened up, yawning.

"We'll have this right out of your way," Brad assured her.

"It's not bothering me. I have a hot date with my pillow."

Hollyn smirked over her shoulder as Nate dragged the flatbed away.

"I don't have to ask if Elsie stuffed you with breakfast. Did she introduce you to any of the cats?"

"I think she wanted to, but I barely kept from falling asleep on my plate." She yawned again. "I apologize…I assure you, it's not the company."

Abashed, Brad stepped aside so she could enter. "I'm sorry…I'm keeping you up. But, um…you know, if you ever want to come and meet the cats, or maybe have a coffee, come on over."

"Oh, I'd love to, but I keep weird hours."

"Me, too. Cats don't keep people schedules. If you

see lights on, come over and knock." He winced.

Suave, Brad.

"I might take you up on that." Maggie mustered a smile. "After I get some sleep."

"And I guess…I'll see you at Community Day?"

That didn't sound at all pathetic, did it?

Maybe not. Maggie's smile deepened. "I guess you will."

The event suddenly seemed much more appealing.

Chapter Three

Maggie rolled over and snuggled into her pillows. A mild autumn breeze ruffled the curtains. After a brief flurry of school buses and trash trucks, the noise level dropped to allow for further snoozing.

Mmm…just an hour or so…

Or until the revving of some sort of mechanical monstrosity shattered the peace. Lawnmower? Leaf blower? Sherman tank? Whatever was causing the racket, every dog in the neighborhood from Cuthbert to the toy poodle next door yammered their displeasure. She yanked a pillow over her head.

Nope. Now I can't breathe.

She flung aside the pillow and sat up, blinking. Stacks of boxes and an overflowing hamper mocked her.

Ugh. Maybe I should let Elsie help me with this disaster. What's a little embarrassment between friends?

The noise level didn't abate, so she slid out of bed and shambled to the kitchen in search of coffee. A card with a little gnome from a Mrs. Morgan a few doors down was stuck to the fridge door with a Tyler Automotive magnet.

Hafta check the house number and stop to say hello. The chaos wasn't so bad in here. Each time Elsie stopped by with food, she somehow whisked a few things into place. As a result, the kitchen almost looked almost like a responsible adult's.

Except responsible adults usually managed to remember to buy coffee when the can was empty. *Fudgebuckets.* Laundry and unpacking without caffeine? Uh-uh. Not happening. A neat stack of Elsie's dishes caught her eye. She had a standing invitation to meet the cats. *Maybe I can return Elsie's dishes and mooch a cup of coffee? Yeah…that sounds like a plan.*

****

One shower and change of clothes later, she stood on Brad's porch. Totes labeled with blue tape and marker stood in neat stacks. Stuff for Community Day, most likely. She sucked in a deep breath and shifted her grip on Elsie's serving plates. She reached for the doorbell with her free hand, then turned the gesture into shoving her hair behind her ear.

Stop. You're not twelve. Ring the stupid bell already.

Brad might not even be home. Which shouldn't matter, anyway. He was a neighbor. Good friend material. That's what she was looking for right now. Besides, Elsie might answer the door herself, take her dishes, and that would be that. Okay…if Elsie came to the door, more food would be forthcoming, but that was good, too, right? Friendship and a little mothering. *Just what I need right now.*

Still, it might be nice to spend time with a friendly, good-looking guy who happened to have a soft spot for animals. And was single, as Elsie had made sure to mention on multiple occasions.

She gave herself a sharp mental shake and pressed the doorbell before she could overthink things anymore. After a long moment, she heard movement in the front hall, and Brad opened the door, a squirming cat—Nixie?—tucked under his arm. He was barefoot, wearing beat-up jeans and a T-shirt proclaiming he "liked cats and maybe three people." Was she imagining things, or did his smile brighten when he recognized her?

"Hi." *Oh, very original, Maggie.* "I have dishes to return to Elsie."

"Come on in."

She stepped inside, noticing things she'd been too exhausted to catch on her last visit. The front entry contained the usual coat rack, boot tray, and umbrella stand. A reception desk with a laptop and clear plastic donation box was sandwiched into the small space and a floor-to-ceiling cat tree housed two residents. They blinked lazily at the new arrival and then went right back to sleep.

Brad nodded at the cat tree. "That's He and Se." He chuckled. "Helium and Selenium. Hollyn perpetrated that one. They're a couple of foster fails who turned up one year during finals. Don't ever let a sleep-deprived science major name anything."

Nixie wriggled from Brad's arms and rubbed against Maggie's ankles. "This is Nixie. Chief Parker rescued her from a pond. Hence the name. A nixie is a water sprite."

Maggie bent to pet her. "Aww…she's darling."

"She's a holy terror. The cute is protective camouflage."

"What's a foster fail?"

"A cat who was intended to be put up for adoption, but someone got too attached."

"Someone?"

Brad ran a lazy hand along one purring ball of tabby fur. "Depends on who you ask. I blame Hollyn, and she blames me."

Maggie straightened and a cluster of framed permits on the wall caught her attention.

Brad grimaced. "Yeah…Mr. Carson tried to sic the health department on me once upon a time."

"Doesn't he have anything better to do?" Nothing but the faint scent of spray cleaner tickled her nose. "This place is immaculate. If I didn't see these guys, I'd never guess there were any animals here."

"That's a testament to lots of elbow grease—mostly Elsie's. The newer staff at town hall mostly write him off as a crank, so he's had to go farther afield for his entertainment."

"Wait—didn't he have an opinion piece in the local paper? The guys stuck it on the dart board in the break room."

Brad rolled his eyes. "That's his annual protest against Community Day. He's a big believer in tradition." He held up his hands and waggled his first two fingers. "I've written books about social justice and society trying to recover from colonialism. He petitioned to have them removed from the local library."

"Nice guy." She shook her head. "And here I thought small towns were all about community and being good neighbors."

His face crinkled into a grin. "We are…more or less."

"Anyway…I thought I'd take you up on your offer of coffee? If I'm not interrupting?"

"Absolutely not—not interrupting, I mean." Brad screwed up his face and bopped himself in the head with one hand. He sucked in a deep breath and tried again. "I mean, please come in, and I'll make a fresh pot."

"Are you sure?" *He's kind of adorable when he's*

flustered.

"Very much so. I've been sitting at the computer for way too long, and the contents of my mug are probably well on the way to becoming penicillin. I'll start fresh coffee, and we can go meet cats while it brews. Sound good?"

He led the way through to the big open-plan kitchen as he spoke. The fixtures and appliances were much more up-to-date than hers. Kid-proof latches and locks secured the stove knobs and cabinets. A tray beneath the bay window held kibble and water bowls, and a large litterbox occupied the corner. Towels, potholders and pretty much every other type of decorative object featured cute cats and kittens. Nixie ran straight to a stack of cases of canned cat food and patted the boxes hopefully.

"Nope. You've already eaten. And don't go turning those eyes on Maggie."

Nixie jumped up on the pile of cat food boxes. She looked from one human to the other, then meowed pitifully and wandered off to sulk.

Maggie spied a set of salt and pepper shakers shaped like kittens wearing costumes. "Elsie?"

He grinned. "I think those were a gift from an adopter. A lot is from my mom." His smile dimmed. "Halloween was her favorite holiday."

"I'm sorry. You must miss her."

He cleared his throat. "I do. I adore Elsie—"

"But no matter how much you love her, she's not the same as your mom. I understand." *I really want to hug him. Is that weird? Or too soon? Maybe. Probably.* She shifted the dishes in her hands. "Is she here today? Elsie, I mean."

25

"Let me grab those. Hmm…two casseroles, cookies, and cupcakes?" he guessed, looking at the assortment. He gestured to the barstools at the island, and she hopped up onto one.

"Um, yeah. I think. Something like that."

"Elsie likes to feed people." He stacked the dishes in the center of the counter. Nixie hopped up to sniff them, and he lifted her down automatically. "I think she's still upstairs, playing with the babies."

She quirked an eyebrow at him. "You don't know who's in your own house?"

He had the grace to look embarrassed as he fiddled with a coffee machine that looked like the same model as the big café chains used. "I tend to be a bit…oblivious to what's going on around me when I'm on a deadline."

"Deadline for what?"

"I write and edit kid's books and sometimes magazine articles."

"Yeah? What about?" She rested her elbows on a Halloween kitty placemat and leaned forward.

He shrugged without interrupting his task. "Whatever my publisher is commissioning. Nature and social studies, mostly. " He finished measuring and pouring and started the machine.

"Do you need an engineering degree to operate that thing?"

"Best investment ever. You would not believe how much coffee we go through around here. This'll take a few minutes. Want to come meet the residents?"

"I'd love to." She slid to her feet, curiosity overcoming the lack of caffeine.

"So—the fifty-cent tour. Kitchen, obviously. The pantry's through there." He indicated a door with a frosted glass panel. "People food to the left and cat supplies to the right."

A large whiteboard mounted on the wall listed the type and quantity of food for each cat, as well as sanitary protocols. Magnets from pet supply companies separated the neat lists of information. A wall calendar from a famous cat rescue in Canada provided an adorable splash of color.

"Elsie must love this."

"Actually, she's been going on about your kitchen."

"But mine's so tiny and…oh—I see. I have a wall oven. So she doesn't have to bend down to lift heavy pans."

"Ah. I wouldn't know. I'm told I eat far too much takeout."

Maggie shrugged. "Me, too."

She followed him up the stairs. Framed photos adorned the walls—a younger Elsie and a woman with Brad's kind eyes and smile. Hollyn holding a first-place New York State science fair ribbon. An adorable tiny Brad under a Christmas tree with his arms wrapped around a cocker spaniel puppy.

In contrast to the open floorplan downstairs, doors lined the upstairs hallway. Three of them had large windows in the center. A small whiteboard and a file holder were mounted on the wall beside each windowed door. Two of the rooms were lit. The third was dark and its file holder was empty. She stepped around a plastic basket one of the residents had tipped over, spilling toys down the hallway. A low bookcase sat between two of the glass doors. A box of latex gloves, one of tissues, and a roll of paper towels secured with a rubber band sat on top, with neatly labeled binders and plastic boxes of supplies filling the shelves.

"This is an amazing setup."

"Thanks. It took me and Hollyn a few years to set up everything the way we wanted—and a lot of fast talking with contractors. Oh, and don't worry…the people rooms have regular doors."

"Good to know." She nudged a couple of balls aside with her foot and wandered over to the first door. A note marked "Live cam & mic," along with the date was stuck on the glass. The whiteboard said "April" in large letters, then smaller underneath: "Sunny," "Rainy," and "Flowers." The room was a cat wonderland, complete with a litter box, feeding station, cat tree, and colorful toys scattered on the floor. A brown tabby mama cat peeked from a cardboard haunted house, watching her three kittens scampering across the floor playing with Elsie.

Brad tapped the glass, and Elsie smiled and waved at them with the wand toy in her hand.

"Is this what she does when she's not feeding people?"

"Yup. Elsie gets the kittens used to being handled and the adults accustomed to being around people. We can't place them for adoption if they don't trust people."

"And she's on camera?"

"Live streaming the kittens is one of the best strategies for a rescue like The Clowder. People all over the world follow us. We get publicity and donations and find good homes for the cats. Elsie's a really good sport about being broadcast over the internet babbling baby talk to kittens."

"She's amazing."

"We couldn't do this without her. I have to spend a

certain amount of time writing because that's what pays the bills, and Hollyn has her practice."

"How did she become involved in this?"

"Elsie was our mom's best friend. We've known her all our lives."

Maggie browsed the file folder for the room. Each resident had their own page. Mama's had her stats from when she was brought in, and there was one for each kitten. "Did your sister design these?"

Brad nodded. "Anything to do with health and safety, she has the final word. Publicity and IT is me."

"Impressive." She replaced the file. "Can we go in?"

"April's still a little cautious about people. She's used to Elsie, but we don't want to press our luck. Come and meet these guys."

He led the way to another door. The sign read "Nebula" and "Cosmos." Inside, two darling half-grown black and white kitties frolicked. The note read "Security cam only." He tapped the yellow sticky note with one finger. "This means the room is only visible on my monitor. I swap the feeds around, so people can see all of them. Carson Mills is hardly the bandwidth capital of the country." He glanced at her feet. "We don't wear shoes in the cat rooms."

"Of course—that makes sense." She leaned on the wall and pulled off her sneakers.

He opened the door, and they slipped inside. "Hey, guys."

Maggie followed, keeping her movements slow and non-threatening.

Brad kneeled, and the two large kittens swarmed him. "This is Nebula." He indicated the spotted "cow kitty." "And this is Cosmos."

The tuxedo with immaculate white gloves and socks fixed his gaze on Maggie and trotted over to sniff her. Delighted, she kneeled and held out her hand. Then, under cover of cuddling her new friend, she observed Brad.

He spoke to the cats in a low and even tone. His smile was warm and unguarded. Her stomach fluttered pleasantly, even though that smile wasn't directed at her. *Jack never looked at anything like that...not even me.*

Cosmos bopped her with his nose, demanding more attention.

"You really love them, don't you?"

"What's not to love?" Brad chuckled. "Ouch. Okay, that. We don't chew on fingers," he informed the unrepentant kitten firmly. He offered a kicker with ribbon streamers instead.

Still kind even while being used for a chew toy. *Does he realize how appealing that is?*

"Where do they come from?"

"I trapped April in the woods. These two turned up in the backyard and made themselves at home. Hollyn and I finally managed to trap them the day the big delivery ended up on your porch."

"How do you know if they're really strays?"

"Well, sometimes it's obvious. Siamese and ragdolls aren't common outdoors. We check every cat we find for microchips, tattoos, or an ear tip. Hollyn posts pictures on the board in her office and compares them to the local lost pets website. Our live streams help, too. I think there was only one time we picked up a bona fide lost pet."

"Did you find their family?"

"We did." He smiled at the memory. "That was a

good day. We've also had a few cats pass through here we suspect were dumped."

Maggie looked up from Cosmos, who'd made himself right at home in her lap. "I'd ask how people can do that, but…I've seen too much stuff."

"Yeah." Brad looked weary. "We can't fix everything, but we try. Cats passing through here receive the medical help they need and a good home if we can possibly manage it."

This is so incredible. And they built it all themselves. How do I even—

The doorbell echoed through the house.

Chapter Four

Brad winced at the sound.

Can't I have one complete conversation? Just one? Would the universe really implode?

"I need to answer that. I'm pretty sure Hollyn isn't lurking around here this morning. And the coffee should be done by now."

He offered Maggie a hand up, and after a brief tussle with Cosmos, they slipped out the door. She scooped up her shoes and followed him downstairs.

"Keep an eye for Nixie, would you?"

"Sure." She leaned against the wall and slipped her sneakers on.

Brad opened the front door to his neighbor Nate and Nate's daughter Mandy. The little girl held something wrapped in an old towel smudged with suspicious reddish brown splotches.

"Hi, Brad. I know this isn't exactly your thing, but Mandy thought maybe you could help."

"Of course. Come on in before—"

Maggie scooped up Nixie as she dodged for the open door.

"Before that." He ushered them inside and shut the door.

"Are you okay, sweetie?" Maggie edged around him, trying to look at the child.

"Nate, this is Maggie Edwards. She's a paramedic."

"We met the other day—sort of. I apologize for my manners, miss."

"No worries. You were upset." Maggie set Nixie down and nudged her into the living room.

"Mandy's fine. Cuthbert was running around in front of my house. When I went to shoo him away, he dropped this." He gestured to whatever his daughter held.

Brad dropped to one knee in front of the little girl. "Mandy, can I see?"

Mandy looked up at her dad, who nodded reassuringly. Then she held out the little wriggling bundle to Brad. He carefully unwrapped a small brown bunny, obviously the worse for its encounter with the dalmatian.

"I don't think Cuthbert meant to hurt the poor thing." Nate half shrugged.

"Probably not. He's not a vicious dog…just hopelessly untrained. I can't tell how badly he's hurt. I'll have my sister take a look."

So much for coffee with the lovely new neighbor.

"It might be kinder for Doc MacKenzie to just…you know." Nate glanced at his daughter.

"I let Hollyn make those decisions." Brad turned his attention to Mandy. "Thanks for bringing me this little guy."

"Can you make him better, like you do with the cats?"

"I'm going to try my very best. I'm going to take him to see my sister. She's an animal doctor, and she has a friend who's very good at taking care of bunnies."

"Thanks, Mr. Brad." She smiled shyly. "You're coming to Community Day, right? It's really important."

"I sure am." Brad stood with the bunny cradled in his hands. "When you get home, you'll want to wash your hands with plenty of soap and hot water. You should always do that if you've touched a wild animal."

"Will do. If I'd realized what Cuthbert had, I would have grabbed a pair of work gloves." Nate fished around in his pocket and deposited a creased and ragged five in the donation box. "Contribution for bunny food."

"Thanks, Nate. That's very kind."

"Please let me know what happens." Nate nodded to Maggie and led his daughter down the path.

****

"Are things always so exciting around here?"

"You have no idea."

Maggie looked at the tiny creature in his hands. He cradled the trembling little furball so gently against his chest—and spoke so kindly to the little girl.

Okay—not the time or the place.

"Does the little guy have a chance?"

"I don't know. I'm going to clean him up and take him over to Hollyn's clinic."

"Can I help? I mean, I don't know animals in particular, but I'm good with triage in general."

Brad grinned at her. "That would be great."

"Kitchen?"

"Actually, no. Basement." He led the way to the stairs. "One of the perks of having an entire house to work with is enough space to not have to treat sick animals in the same place as we eat."

"Smart."

Brad led her down a flight of steps and past a washer, drier, and slop sink, to a wide, sturdy counter. Cabinets above the counter held supplies. Pet carriers and live traps were stacked neatly beneath.

"Wow."

One corner of his mouth quirked up. "Again, anything logical, thank Hollyn. Can you hold him while I grab some things?"

"Sure." She snagged a pair of gloves from the box on the counter, then accepted the towel-cocooned rabbit.

"Thanks. I don't think he's strong enough to bolt, but I've been wrong before, and I don't want to waste time tearing the place apart, trying to catch him."

Maggie peeled back the corner of the towel and saw two tiny bright eyes peering at her. "Hey, little guy. How are you doing?" The bunny, of course, didn't answer, but he seemed to enjoy being cuddled.

Brad quickly collected a couple of washcloths and a towel. He wrung out a washcloth in warm water and then slipped on his own gloves.

"This doesn't look like enough blood for a fatal injury." Maggie flushed. "I mean, I don't know bunnies, but…"

"Probably not. Like I said, Cuthbert isn't vicious, and he isn't starving. He has zero manners and no idea of his own strength. I'm going to clean this little fella so I have an idea of what we're dealing with."

"What do you want me to do?"

"Can you hold him, so he doesn't wiggle away?"

"Sure."

He opened the towel, and Maggie adjusted her grip on the little creature. The critter was tiny, so personal space went right out the window. Not that she particularly objected. She might not be in the market for a new boyfriend, but she wasn't dead after all. Brad was easy on the eyes, and his voice was low as he soothed the trembling bunny with a steady stream of nonsense. Warmth radiated from him, along with a clean, pleasant scent of soap. Maggie didn't care much for heavy cologne on men, but she was even less fond of stink. She got enough of that at the firehouse, thanks very much.

Brad gently sponged dirt and blood off the little furball to determine the extent of his injuries. "Um…I should have asked this before I let you hold him, but your tetanus shot is up to date, right?"

"Yup. I've even gotten the rabies vaccine."

He quirked an eyebrow at that bit of information.

"Long story, involving bats."

"I like bats."

"Not in those circumstances, you wouldn't." She shuddered. "What do you think?" She leaned her arms on the counter, peering at their little patient.

"Well, Hollyn will make the final call, but I don't think any of the bites are too deep. I think Cuthbert used the poor thing for a toy."

"So, more shock and fear than actual trauma?"

"That would be my guess. Um…I'm sorry about the coffee."

"Raincheck?"

Brad focused on the bunny, then turned his head to look at her. "Unless…do you want to ride into town with me? There's a good diner near the clinic. They make amazing pie."

"Hmm…fresh coffee and fresh baked goods? You sure know how to charm a girl. Who's driving?"

"I will. Let me pop him into a carrier, and we'll go."

Her smile turned sly. "One more thing."

"What's that?"

"Shoes?"

Startled, he looked at his bare feet, then threw back his head and laughed. "Shoes," he agreed.

"Car keys, maybe?"

Chapter Five

"So, how was your date?" Elsie slid a crumb bun in front of Brad.

Se's nose twitched, and she cracked her eyes open.

Brad choked and nearly spewed a mouthful of coffee across the papers spread out on the counter. "My what?"

"Your date." Elsie covered the rest of the buns with an orange and black plaid dish towel. "You know—that thing where you took Maggie for a ride into town to the diner."

"That was not a date. Look, she came over to return the dishes from all the food you made for her. We were gonna have coffee—"

"I noticed. I dumped the pot out before anyone was poisoned."

"I meant to—"

Without seeming to move, Se somehow sidled a bit closer to Brad's plate.

"Did you give her a tour of the house?"

"Well, yeah, while the coffee was brewing. She was interested. In the cats," he stressed, seeing the smug grin on her face.

"There's nothing wrong with her eyesight—or mine, for that matter. She's interested in more than the cats."

"You're imagining things. For one thing, we just

met."

Elsie continued unloading the dishwasher. "So, you should have another date to get to know each other better."

"It was not a date. It was coffee. Which we were going to have here—nice and casual and not remotely date-like, until the neighbors showed up on my doorstep with a bunny Cuthbert used for a chew toy. Which is quite possibly the least romantic incident of my life."

"So instead, you went into town, to the diner, where you paid the tab for both of you."

"We went into town to take the bunny to Hollyn's clinic, and then I took Maggie for coffee to thank her for her help." He caught a flicker of movement from the corner of his eye, but when he turned his head, Se had both paws tucked neatly underneath her chest.

"And what did you talk about over coffee?" Elsie frowned at a spot on a plate and grabbed a dishtowel to polish away the offending smudge.

"I dunno…lots of things."

"Like?"

"Like our jobs and—and—stuff." *Will you focus already? You need to finish proofing this project and return the files to Frank if you wanna be paid. And why is Elsie still going on about me and Maggie?*

"You mean the things people talk about on a first date."

"Yes. I guess. No—not a date of any sort."

Elsie stared at him with a self-satisfied smile playing over her features.

"And how do you know about this anyway?"

"Brad MacKenzie, you've lived in this town your entire life. You know quite well, if you want to know the news, you don't turn on the TV—you pop into the diner."

Brad cringed. *I really should have known better.*

Elsie's expression softened. "You may find this hard to believe, but folks in this town are fond of their Cat Guy. They like the idea of you finding a nice young lady to spend time with."

"And by folks, you mean…?"

"Well, Millie waited on you, so I'm sure she told Gail when she ran your card through the register, and one of them would have told Charlie, the fry cook—" She stooped and fished Nixie out of the dishwasher.

"—Who would have told Gus who washes the windows at half the businesses on Main Street. So basically the whole town, at this point. Great. Look…I know you mean well, but I'm not looking to get involved with anyone."

"You haven't been looking to get involved with anyone the entire time I've known you."

"You've known me my whole life."

"My point exactly."

Brad heaved a sigh. "Yeah, well, these guys take up an awful lot of time. Then there's my actual paying job." Speaking of which, he shifted papers around the counter—his red pen was right—on the floor. He stretched down and snatched the pen away from Nixie, who looked very put-out.

"Lots of people have jobs and interests and still find time to be with someone."

"I'm not lots of people. I like my life the way it is. I'm not going to change to suit someone else's expectations."

"I don't think you give that young lady near enough credit."

"I've been through this too many times, all right? Guys are only allowed to write tough, manly books about spies or detectives. And we're only allowed to like dogs and maybe horses. Kids' books and cats make me—"

"A fine, upstanding, compassionate gentleman."

Brad snorted.

"Why are you so sure someone so dedicated to helping others doesn't find those qualities attractive?"

"Maggie is gorgeous and funny and smart, and she can have her pick of the entire county fire department."

"And if she wanted any of those guys, she'd be with one of them already."

"Elsie…look, I'm not that guy, okay? I'm not the one women want to date. I'm the one women call when that guy's had one too many, and they need rescuing."

"Exactly. You're a gentleman. I don't know why you think that's so undervalued."

"Why are you so set on this?"

"Because you're two very nice people who could be very good for one another. You just need to get your head out of your—"

"Elsie!"

She stepped in closer and laid a hand on his arm. "You have an enormous heart, with room for every living thing that needs your help. All I'm saying is, make sure you leave room for yourself. Now, I'm going to go feed April and the babies. Eat your bun." She lifted Se off the counter and set her on the floor.

****

Maggie wandered into the diner in search of…well, whatever you called the meal when you realized you were starving at three in the afternoon. There was a poster for Community Day taped inside the front window. The bell over the door jingled when she entered, and a breath of warm, coffee-and-brownie-scented air wafted around her. *Real food first.*

Kitschy black and orange crepe paper decorations dangled from the ceiling, swaying with every stray puff of air. The local cable station played on the TV mounted above the counter and a hum of conversation buzzed over the chink of silverware on thick, ceramic dishes. She spotted Hollyn seated at the counter and hopped onto the next stool. Gail waved from the register and grabbed a water glass from under the counter.

"Hollyn, hi. How's the bunny?"

Hollyn wiped her lips with a paper napkin and gulped whatever was in her mouth. "Hey, Maggie. My friend Cody's looking after him. He's a licensed wildlife rehabilitator. He's going to take him to the nature center to be part of the education program."

"I'm glad." Gail set a glass of water in front of her, and Maggie grabbed the drink and took a sip. "When we first saw him…well…I wasn't sure there was going to be a happy ending."

"How did you come to be mixed up in the whole thing?"

"Dumb luck. I had a sort of open-ended invitation to meet cats and have coffee. I also had a bunch of serving plates and containers to return to Elsie." Gail passed her a menu with one hand and gestured with the coffee pot in the other.

Hollyn chuckled and nudged her mug forward for a refill. "Yeah, she does love to feed people." She eyed Maggie speculatively. "So…you and my brother."

Maggie added a packet of sugar to her mug and reached for the cream. "Me and your brother, what?"

"You rescued a bunny together, then went for coffee."

"Well…I suppose…I mean, we just met. It was coffee." She barely caught herself from letting the cream overflow her mug.

"Coffee is good." Hollyn took a sip from her own mug. "Half of my brother's total blood volume is composed of coffee."

"Look…I think maybe you're reading too much into this. We're neighbors. Friends, maybe? We just met, and honestly…I'm not…you know…looking to become involved with anyone right now."

"Sometimes, that's when you find the right person."

"Your brother is a terrific guy, but really…I worked my tail off to earn my certification. I'm the only female paramedic in the department. This isn't the sort of job that stops for weekends and holidays and date nights." She paused a moment. "And…look, I didn't move here because of my job. I mean, I did. I wanted a quiet place to rest and relax on my days off. But I also just broke up with someone. He didn't think my job was as important as supporting his."

Hollyn took one final swig of coffee, then set down her mug and spun on her stool to face Maggie. "I know what it's like to have a career you worked very hard for that doesn't follow a nine-to-five schedule. I'm pretty sure my brother likes you. I know for an absolute fact he'll respect the way you choose to live your life. Don't be so quick to discount the possibility, okay?"

"Okay," Maggie finally replied after a long moment.

Hollyn's phone buzzed, and she checked the display. "Gotta go." She laid a twenty on the counter and slipped from her stool. "See you Saturday?"

Maggie nodded. "Stop by the blood drive tent, if you dare." She caught a flash of movement out of the corner of her eye and realized Gail stood by pencil poised to take her order. And probably report the entire conversation to the rest of the staff.

Yay for small-town life.

****

Maggie wasn't surprised to find Brad on her doorstep later that evening. He leaned against the porch rail, and she noticed some peeling paint. *Gotta mention that to my landlord before old Mr. Carson reports him to town hall.*

"Hi, Maggie." He held out the covered plate in his hands. "Elsie made crumb buns. We managed to save a couple for you."

She grinned and took the plate. "If she keeps this up, I might have to go on a diet."

"You don't need to…I mean…you look terrific."

Her cheeks flushed. "Thanks." Distraction, distraction…she settled on today's T-shirt, which featured an orange cat. "Nice shirt."

He grinned. "From a fundraiser for a rescue in New Jersey. We try to support each other's efforts." He shoved his hands in his pockets. "So…um…since we're both working on Community Day, I was wondering…can you take breaks?"

"I imagine so. I mean, the blood drive runs all-day."

"So maybe we could walk around and see the town? Grab a bite to eat?"

"That sounds great."

Chapter Six

Brad stopped at the barricade surrounding the town square and opened his window.

" 'Morning, Mr. MacKenzie," one of Chief Parker's deputies greeted him with a broad grin. He consulted his clipboard. "All the nonprofits are together. The Clowder is in tent number six, right in front of town hall."

Brad blinked. "Um…okay. Wow. Wasn't expecting that."

"You can pull right up to unload, but all vehicles must clear the area by nine thirty."

"Will do."

"Enjoy the festival, sir." The deputy stepped aside and waved him through.

"Who'd we bribe for such a great placement?"

Hollyn snickered. "Wouldn't you like to know? I hope we didn't get the tent with the wasp nest."

"I'm pretty sure they took care of it, Hollyn. That was three years ago."

She shuddered. "A swarm of angry wasps isn't the sort of thing you forget."

People waved and called out greetings as Brad maneuvered the SUV through the early morning crowd. Neat rows of pop-up tents lined the square, food on one side and crafts opposite. Non-profits and service organizations were lined up in a row in front of the town hall, the courthouse, and the library. Vendors and volunteers unloaded in front of their respective tents, dodging little kids, frisbees, and balls. Families set up lawn chairs and picnic blankets on the green around the gazebo and war memorials.

"Why is everyone smiling at me?" Brad checked his reflection in the rearview mirror. *Nope. Nothing stuck in my teeth.*

"They're happy. People do that."

"I'm starting to feel like I'm in one of those villages that's been taken over by aliens or something."

Hollyn huffed. "Brad. Can you just accept that today's a beautiful day, we're gonna have a great festival, and people are happy?"

"Not this happy." He waved at yet another smiling neighbor. "This is creepy."

"Old man Carson lost his bid to return to the bad old days of celebrating colonialism and slavery. It's enough to make anyone smile."

Brad parked in front of the tent marked number six. Prime real estate, right at the foot of the steps of the town hall. "Nope. People look snarky when they've one-upped Mr. Carson. Everyone just looks…happy. Like happy-happy." He popped the hatch and climbed from the SUV.

The mayor's wife bustled over, clutching a clipboard in her hands and a megaphone under her arm. "Mr. MacKenzie, Dr. MacKenzie—welcome. This is your spot today. Now, remember, you need to move your vehicle by nine thirty."

"Yes, ma'am. The deputy told us." Brad hefted plastic totes from the trunk and transferred them to the tent.

"You have a table and three chairs—I hope you brought a table skirt?"

"We did." Hollyn grabbed the plastic-swathed hanger from the passenger side coat hook.

"Good. The kids from the varsity basketball team are hanging things, and the football players are helping with any heavy lifting."

"That's great." Hollyn slid a rolled-up banner from the back seat.

"Here—let me give you a hand with that." The First Lady grabbed one end of the banner and helped maneuver it to the table. "I can't tell you how happy we are to have you with us today. I'll send a couple of the boys to hang that for you." Then she caught sight of portly Mr. Melville balancing precariously on a folding table trying to hang his own banner. "Oh, dear…let me just…" She trotted off in the direction of imminent disaster, speaking urgently into a walkie-talkie.

"Brad MacKenzie, I thought I told you to wear a good shirt."

He winced. "My shirt's in the car, Elsie. I'll change after I finish setting up."

"See that you do." She straightened her pristine golf shirt embroidered with The Clowder's logo and tucked a wisp of faded blonde hair behind her ear. "Now, what can I do to help?"

"You can sort the giveaways." Hollyn set a stack of plastic baskets on the table. Her shirt looked like she— or one of the cats—had slept in it—not that Elsie commented on *her* appearance.

"What do we have this time?"

Hollyn fished a couple of smaller totes from under the back seat. "Pencils for the kids—they can just have those—why do we have such a truly insane amount, anyway?"

"Because pencils don't go bad, everyone can use them, and the price per unit was cheaper the more I ordered." Brad wrestled a heavier box out of the car. "The bowls and pooper scoopers are for cash donations, and the T-shirts are for sale."

Feedback screeched from the megaphone. "Folks, this is your fifteen-minute reminder: all vehicles need to be cleared from the square and the parade route."

Brad set down a cooler and glanced around the tent. "Anything else we need to toss in the car?"

"I think we're good," Hollyn decided. "We can push the empty totes under the table. Go park the car, then come back and help us make the tent pretty."

"And change your shirt."

He rolled his eyes. "Elsie, you know I'm not in your classroom anymore, right? And this isn't school picture day?"

She faced him with her hands on her hips "Brad MacKenzie, long before you were in my classroom, I changed your diapers."

Could she say that any louder?

"Now go change your shirt."

He sighed. "Yes, Elsie."

"Comb your hair, too," Hollyn added.

He paused halfway into the car. "Seriously?"

What's gotten into everyone today?

****

The squawk and clatter of bands warming up filled the air, along with the occasional whoop of a siren. Maggie took advantage of the walk from their distant parking spot to browse the eclectic mix of storefronts. All the shops had posters for Community Day prominently displayed.

The bookstore's window featured spooky stories, both classic and new. A chocolatier displayed vintage tin candy molds interspersed with gold foil boxes tied with chocolate brown velvet ribbon. A new-age shop wasn't something that would ordinarily catch her eye, but this one had a sparkling display of crystals and geodes, supervised by a magnificent long-haired gray cat. Maybe a former resident of The Clowder? *I'll have to ask Brad.*

And then she rounded the corner and stopped dead in her tracks. Ted plowed into her, and she stumbled over the edge of a set of sidewalk cellar doors that bonged and clanked under her feet.

"Jeez, Mags—it's not like anything's open today." He caught her elbow with his free hand. "Watch where you're…oh. Hi, Brad."

She yanked her arm free of Ted's grasp. Heat blazed her cheeks. Brad turned in the act of pulling a fresh shirt into place.

"Maggie." His eyes flickered to her partner. "And…um…"

"Ted," he supplied, grinning like a cat who got into the cream.

"Ted. Right. Hi." Brad tugged his shirt straight, then gave his hair a half-hearted swipe.

Is he happy to see me? Or am I reading too much into things?

"Gotta look good for your big moment." Ted smirked.

"What big moment?"

Maggie elbowed her partner. "The big moment when I stick a needle in your arm." She gestured at her blood drive T-shirt. "You're planning to stop by our tent today, right?"

Brad glanced between the two of them. "Um, sure. Of course, I am."

"You won't feel a thing," Maggie promised him. She straightened his collar, her hands lingering on the soft cotton.

Ted snorted and stepped around them, dragging a red wagon full of supplies. There was the vague sound of a megaphone announcement, but the crisp autumn breeze carried off the words.

"We probably should get going."

Do we really have to? This is so nice, just the two of us... "Right." Maggie dropped her hands and stepped away. "So…how does this work?"

Brad slammed the door of his SUV and stuffed the keys in his pocket. He matched his pace to hers as they strolled to the square. "The parade steps off at ten. It really doesn't take long. The mayor makes a speech and declares the festival open. Then people spend the rest of the day eating and shopping—"

"And visiting the vampires."

"No, that's at the end of the month." He eyed her with a crooked smile, and she swatted at his arm.

"Today's blood drive is important. The County supplies are very low for a couple of blood types."

"Well, you're so much better looking than the usual crew, you'll probably double…oh, crud…" He flushed scarlet. "I shouldn't have said that. I was way out of line. You're a trained professional and I—"

"It's fine." Her mouth curled in the barest hint of a smirk. "Really."

Her eyes widened as they stepped into the square. Cornstalks tied with sparkly orange ribbon festooned the lamp posts. The large concrete planters on the sidewalks overflowed with vibrant red and gold and orange mums. More encircled the etched granite war memorials on the green. Bunches of brown and orange and gold balloons swayed in the breeze. "This is amazing. The stores at the mall already have Halloween squished into a corner somewhere to make room for Christmas." The salt-sweet scent of kettle corn wafted on the breeze. Her mouth watered, even though she'd scarfed a bagel at the station.

Brad chuckled. "We like our seasons here. Some store owners come in to put up their Christmas decorations on Thanksgiving—"

"What, on the actual day?" That didn't really jive with the whole small-town-loves-their-holidays vibe.

"Keeps them out from underfoot of whoever's cooking dinner."

"Oh, gotcha."

"The town's official tree lighting isn't until December first—whatever day that falls on."

"That sounds great. I—"

"Hey, Mags!"

"Brad, will you get your butt over here?"

"I guess duty calls," Brad muttered, scrubbing a hand behind his neck.

"Yeah." Maggie turned toward the blood drive tent.

"Come watch the parade with us once you're finished setting up. We have the best viewing spot."

****

"Are you having fun?" Brad asked.

Maggie sipped her hot chocolate and bumped her shoulder against his. "I am. I always thought you could see a parade better on TV, but it's cool to be in the middle of everything."

Elsie sat in a deluxe camp chair with arms and a cup

holder. No one chose to remark on the fact the back of the chair was stamped "Property of CMPD." Or that Chief Parker set it up for her. That left The Clowder's third folding chair free for Maggie.

Their tent occupied the optimal viewing spot. The local cable station set up on the steps of town hall to capture the performances for posterity—and proud parents. People stopped to chitchat and offer munchies as if she'd lived here all her life.

The sound of a Sousa march grew increasingly closer, and Chief Parker and his deputies shooed the last few stragglers onto the sidewalk. A fire department color guard led the parade, followed by a lovingly restored antique fire engine. Its glossy red paint and brass fittings were spit-shined to a mirror finish. The driver wore a dark cloth uniform with shiny brass buttons and a tall helmet. Two adorable twin girls wearing old-timey ruffled calico dresses took turns ringing the bell.

"That's the first fire engine Carson Mills owned that wasn't pulled by horses," Brad supplied. "It leads off every parade."

"It's gorgeous."

"The town stores it over at the old firehouse. John and Marty at Tyler Automotive provide the upkeep. They also own the convertibles you'll see later."

"Oh, I know the Tylers—they're my downstairs neighbors."

The high school marching band and cheerleaders followed the fire engine. The tuba player was so entranced with the baton twirler he wandered off course and a couple of helpful parents steered him back in line. A wave of laughter rippled through the crowd, and the poor kid's face turned scarlet.

Maggie cringed in sympathy.

"The joys of teenage hormones," Brad muttered.

"Shush," Elsie scolded. "You were both young once."

A couple of shiny green tractors from the Bobbins and Apples Orchard and Country Store pulled hay wagons. The first carried the nominees for Harvest Queen, smiling and waving graciously. The second promoted Halloween events at the local schools. Ghosts and goblins rode on top, tossing candy to the crowd. Kids swarmed the edge of the street, hoping to catch some sweets.

Maggie accepted a bright orange flier from a vampire who could have stalked right off a flight from Transylvania. She scanned the list of events and pointed to the description of the haunted house at the high school gym. "This looks fun."

"Oh, it is. Maybe we could—"

She winced as the skirl of bagpipes drowned out Brad's words. The county pipe and drum corps played an accompaniment for the kids from the local step dancing school. The little ones hopped around in matching green velvet frocks with an adorable excess of energy. Then the parade stopped momentarily while the senior students gave a dazzling demonstration.

She leaned in to speak in Brad's ear. "I didn't realize feet could move so fast."

"Pretty amazing, aren't they? Some of them travel to competitions all over the state."

Hollyn leaned in from the other side. "They have adult classes, too. Lots of fun, but man—what a workout."

Maggie nodded as the kids bowed and scampered

off with varying degrees of composure.

The band followed, except for one solitary piper. He played "Green Fields of France" and a respectful hush descended as the local veterans' group marched past town hall. Two ladies—elderly, but alert and proudly wearing their decorations—rode in the back of a glossy cotton candy pink vintage Italian convertible.

"They're nurses who served in the Korean War," Brad explained. The car paused, and two of the dancers returned to present the ladies with bouquets. "Veteran's Day is usually too cold for them to be outside for too long."

"And Memorial Day is too warm?" she guessed.

He nodded.

The veterans moved on, with the piper pacing after. The state university band and dance team followed. The mayor's open car—a blue convertible with tailfins straight out of a fifties teeny-bopper movie—brought up the rear.

Maggie shaded her eyes to see better. "Why're all those people following the car?"

"The mayor's going to make a speech, officially opening the festival. Then the food goes on sale."

"I guess I should head back to my own tent before they come looking for me."

"Nah, you're good for a few minutes. Nothing starts until after the speech."

"Stay," Hollyn added, "you don't want to miss this."

"Miss what?" Brad demanded.

"You'll see." Elsie placidly sipped tea from a travel mug.

The big, open car glided to a stop in front of town hall and the mayor and her wife got out hand in hand.

Their hair and makeup somehow made Community Day T-shirts and jeans look like photoshoot-worthy ensembles. They smiled and waved while a couple of techs from the news crew ran a final sound check.

"Wow. I'm guessing Mr. Carson didn't vote for her."

Hollyn leaned in. "He tried to have the election overturned."

"Shh," Elsie hissed.

Mayor Alice Roman stepped up behind the podium and beamed at the assembled crowd. "Good morning, everyone. I'm so pleased to see so many of you here on this beautiful day to enjoy the Carson Mills third annual Community Day parade and festival." She paused for the scattered applause and cheers. "As many of you know, Community Day is a fairly new concept, and the committee, headed by my lovely wife, Marisol—take a bow, honey—has been working on ways to make the day a true celebration of our town." More applause, louder this time. "To that end, we organized a series of fundraisers in the town schools. The beneficiary is one of our town's best-known and loved not-for-profit organizations. Can I ask Mr. Brad MacKenzie of The Clowder to join me?"

Whoops and cheers echoed from the crowd now. Brad looked a bit shell-shocked. Maggie squeezed his arm. Elsie and Hollyn shoved him forward. He walked to the podium, a smile plastered on his face.

Mayor Roman smiled and continued. "Mr. MacKenzie—our very own Cat Guy—has worked hard to make The Clowder one of the most respected cat rescues in this part of the country. Last spring was an exceptionally busy kitten season, and it came to our attention The Clowder didn't possess an incubator of its own. They're very clever folks, and they improvised with heating lamps and such, but if they really needed an incubator, they had to borrow one from another facility. We decided that simply wouldn't do. So with the advice of Dr. Hollyn MacKenzie, the children of our town raised funds and purchased this for The Clowder. So folks, all those brownies and candy bars and raffle tickets—this is what they were for."

She gestured, and two cheerleaders presented Brad with a large carton, topped with an extravagant red bow. He still looked stunned—adorably so.

"I don't know what to say. Thank you all so much." He shook the Mayor's hand.

She wrapped both hands around his, turning them to face the cameras. "You keep up the fine work you and your organization do, Mr. MacKenzie. Now, I'd like to declare the festival officially open. Have a great day, folks."

Brad returned to the tent amidst a flurry of handshakes and backslaps. He narrowed his eyes at Hollyn. "How long have you known about this?"

She grinned. "You heard the lady. All summer."

People crowded around the table now, dropping cash in the donation box or chatting with Elsie. The cable news team headed their way, likely for an interview.

Maggie figured no one would notice in the bustle of attention, so she stretched up and planted a kiss on his cheek. "I really do need to go back to my tent now."

Brad finally tore his eyes from the state-of-the-art incubator now sitting on The Clowder's table. "I…um…"

"I'll see you for lunch?" She smiled and touched his

arm.

"Yeah. Lunch."

****

Maggie stole glances at The Clowder's tent throughout the morning. Brad looked more at ease now, accepting donations and chatting with people. One of the candidates for the school board stopped to shake his hand.

"He's a good guy," Ted observed, reaching around her for a fresh pair of gloves.

She shot him a look, and he stepped away, hands raised.

"I'm just saying—we're not all jerks. He's nice, he's single, and he lives across the street."

"Ted—"

"And will ya look at that—he's headed right this way."

"To give blood, Ted. That's what we're here for."

She glanced around the tent. The mayor and her wife rested in lounge chairs, sipping juice, hopefully out of earshot. Brad accepted a clipboard from the volunteer at the front table and started his paperwork. He spotted her and waved.

Ted glanced from one to the other and grinned. "I'll go check on the First Ladies. Might even have a loud and detailed discussion about the weather."

"You know, you're a paramedic, not a matchmaker."

He winked. "Who says I can't be both?"

"Me." She lobbed a balled-up paper wrapper at the back of his head.

"Maggie?"

She pasted on her best professional smile and turned

to face Brad.

"Um…hi. Is this a bad time?" He held out his clipboard.

"There's no such thing as a bad time to donate blood. Come on inside." She glanced at his paperwork. "You've never given blood before?"

He took a seat on one of the lounge chairs. "Nope. First time for everything, I guess."

Maggie perched on the stool beside him. "Well, donating blood is nothing to be nervous about. I'm really good, and I promise I won't hurt you." She slipped on a pair of gloves and set up her supplies.

"Hey, the cats claw me on a regular basis." He fidgeted slightly as she swabbed his arm.

"Relax. Eyes on me, okay? Don't look at your arm and don't look at the bag. Just me."

His face crinkled into a smile. "I think I can manage that."

Chapter Seven

Ted wandered over to check Brad's pulse. "How're you feeling? Any dizziness? Nausea?"

"I'm good, thanks."

"Well, in that case, you're cleared to leave, and we thank you for your time and you know…blood."

"Um…"

"Make sure you leave the bandage on for at least six hours. If you start to feel lightheaded or fatigued, sit until you feel steady. If you don't feel better in a few minutes, send someone here for help." Ted made a show of checking his watch. "Would you look at that? Lunchtime. You should grab something to eat, maybe sit in the shade for a while." As he spoke, Ted escorted him from the tent.

Brad blinked in the sunlight, a bit bemused, then headed for The Clowder's tent.

"Brad."

He stopped and waited for Maggie to catch up.

"Hey, you forgot your sticker and your follow-up instructions." She handed him a printed paper, then affixed a heart-shaped donor sticker to his shirt. Her warm hand lingered on his chest for a moment, smoothing the decal.

"Your friend said I was done and should go grab some lunch."

"My friend?"

He gestured vaguely at his head. "The guy with the scarecrow hair?"

She pressed her lips together. "I am going to murder him."

"Maybe that's a little excessive?" He tried not to grin.

Two spots of bright crimson blossomed on her cheeks. "He said—never mind—he really needs to mind his own business."

Brad looked at his shoes, then back at her. "Maybe, but since we're halfway to the food tents, why don't we grab lunch?"

She linked her arm through his. "We could do that."

He glanced at her sidewise. "You know, if we were to see one of the high school coaches, we could mention you have a quota to meet today."

"I like the way you think." She bumped her shoulder against his.

****

"How are you settling in?" Brad offered her the container of fries.

Maggie helped herself to a few. They were the thick kind, with the skin on, dusted with the perfect amount of salt. *Sooo good. And so bad for my waistline.* "I like the town a lot. Someday I might even finish unpacking."

Brad chuckled. "Yeah…Elsie keeps threatening to go over and put everything away for you."

"I should probably let her. At the rate I'm going, I'll still have stuff in boxes if I ever decide to move again." She shuddered. "Not that I plan on doing this again as long as I live."

"Good. I mean…I like having you for a neighbor."

She glanced at him through her lashes. "Likewise.

Some things take a little getting used to, though."

"Like what?"

She huffed out a small, annoyed sigh. "Like nothing's open twenty-four hours. I'm used to being able to grab a burger or run into a store if I need something, no matter what time my shift ends. Now I have to remember to stop before I get on the thruway."

"Hmm...I grew up here. I guess I never thought about when places are open or closed. I mean, nothing's officially twenty-four hours, but places always seem to be open when someone really needs something. Like when there's an emergency—no matter what time— Charlie keeps the diner open. There's always coffee and sandwiches, and a comfy spot for folks to sit and sort themselves. Or if there's a flu bug or something going around, the family who owns the pharmacy will deliver anything, any time."

Maggie took another bite of her burger and barely caught a drip of sauce with her napkin. "This is a million times better than fast food."

"Best barbecue in town." Brad crunched into his pickle.

"And there's how much competition?"

"Okay, but really, you have to go during the summer. They make burgers and stuff for events like this, but they have a full setup with a barbecue pit at the brewery. Pig roasts, even." He rubbed at the bandage on his arm.

"Does your arm hurt?"

"Huh? No, it's fine."

"Then don't touch the bandage."

"Yes, ma'am."

She wiped her hands, then took a deep swig of ice-cold cider. "But really…how are you? You seemed kind of…I don't know…flustered…this morning."

Brad wiped his mouth and collected the trash onto his paper plate. "I was surprised, is all. I've always been kinda shy. I can deal with the public if I'm prepared—like today, I knew once we opened, I'd be speaking to people. Fine. I don't do well being blindsided, and Hollyn knows that."

"It was a really nice thing, though. Buying the incubator for you."

"True. I've had my eye on one for a while. It's going to save a lot of little lives. Did I look too awful?"

"No. Not at all. Maybe a bit shell-shocked."

Brad stood and extended a hand for her. His fingers wrapped around hers in a warm grip and he tugged her to her feet. "Do we have time for an ice cream?"

"If the ice cream is as good as everything else, we'll make time."

****

Dusk was falling and there was a definite nip in the air when Brad hefted the last—considerably lighter—tote out of the car and added it to the stack on the front porch. "How'd we do today?"

Hollyn transferred the totes inside, using them to push He and Se away from the open door. "We got a bunch of applications for April and the babies. The donation box is stuffed, and I think we're out of most T-shirt sizes."

"We can tally everything tomorrow."

She shivered in the early evening breeze. "I'm beat. I'm gonna feed the monsters and fall into bed."

"I hear you." He shut the hatch and locked the car.

A grunt and a slight scuffle ensued from the porch.

"Oh, no you don't." Hollyn scooped up Nixie before she could escape.

"Shut the door. I'm way too tired to go chasing her down the street." Brad eyeballed the totes left on the porch—nothing valuable or edible. In other words, nothing that couldn't wait until morning.

Crickets chirped—pretty much the only sound in the neighborhood. Parents had herded—or carried—sleepy kids inside a while ago. The Rogers boys tinkered with spooky lights in their front yard, but most people were ready to put their feet up. Maggie's car pulled up in front of the Adams place, and Cuthbert let loose with a flurry of barking.

Maggie saw Brad standing there and waved, so after a glance to make sure Hollyn had indeed gone inside, he shoved his hands in his pockets and strolled across the street. "How was your first Community Day?"

"Wonderful." She paused, yawning. "Excuse me. Exhausting, but wonderful. We turned away a few people at the end of the day."

"That's outstanding."

"The lady who made the thank-you cookies—"

"Jill?"

"I guess? I met so many people today. Anyway, she gave me a couple when we were breaking down. Want one?"

"Ooh, I never pass up one of Jill's cookies." *Or more time with Maggie.* He followed her up the steps and they settled onto the porch swing, which creaked slightly under their weight.

"Mr. Carson was conspicuous by his absence."

Brad snorted. "Not like anyone missed him. He probably spent the day trimming his lawn with manicure scissors while Cuthbert rampaged through the neighborhood. I'm sure we'll find evidence tomorrow. And I can pretty much guarantee he'll be up at the crack of dawn running his leaf blower."

"Earplugs are wonderful things."

He unwrapped his cookie and took a bite. Maggie unwrapped hers, but paused, admiring the elaborate icing.

"This is almost too pretty to eat."

"Trust me, that cookie is too good *not* to eat."

Maggie responded with a very satisfied, somewhat muffled *mmm*. She finished chewing and swiped at her mouth with her fingers. "The day was well organized. I thought the mayor said this was only the third one?"

"Well, there's always been a parade and street fair. We just changed the subject three years ago. We stopped talking about a questionable person from five hundred years ago and put the focus on the folks who live in our community now. Most of us are happy with the way the festival turned out."

Maggie leaned her head against his shoulder, and they sat in companionable silence for a few minutes. A breeze rustled the fallen leaves, and the swing squeaked as they rocked back and forth. A low murmur of a televised car race drifted from the Tyler's open window behind them.

"I had a really great day."

Brad slipped a tentative arm around her. "I'm glad."

"Did I really see Elsie and Chief Parker together?"

"Yeah. They've been friends forever."

"Friends? Are you sure about that?"

"I guess. I mean, she was my high school English teacher, so it's a little weird to think of her like that."

Maggie snuggled a little closer into his side. "I never realized there was so much right here in town. I want to go to the orchard and the brewery, and I want to walk around the square when those cute shops are open."

Brad's heart sped up. Here was his opening…if he had the guts to reach for it.

"Actually…I was wondering…you seemed to like the diner…would you like to go for dinner? Or lunch? Whatever works for you."

She tipped her head up and her lips curved into a smile. "I'm off on Tuesday."

"Tuesday's good."

"Just…not too early?"

A relieved grin spread over his features. "How about you come over whenever you're ready? My schedule's pretty flexible."

"And you'll be wearing shoes and everything?"

He glanced away, then back to her, chuckling. "Worst case scenario, you can play with the cats for a few minutes while I finish something up. Scout's honor."

They yawned simultaneously.

"Sorry—"

"It's been a—"

"Long day," they concluded in chorus.

Brad unfolded himself from the swing and pulled Maggie up. He didn't want to let go of her hands yet. The light over the front door illuminated the sparkle in her green eyes and a delicate pink blush on her cheeks. He leaned down—or maybe she leaned up—did it really matter? Their noses bumped and then her lips brushed the corner of his mouth.

"G'night, Brad. I'll see you Tuesday."

"Tuesday." *How many days is that? Too many.* He

watched while she stepped inside and waited until he heard the click of the front door lock.

****

Maggie locked the front door and leaned against it. Her lips still tingled from the kiss. Wait—did it even count as a kiss?

Hello? Your lips, his lips? Yes, it counts as a kiss.

"Goodnight, Maggie," Marty Tyler called through the closed front door of their unit.

"Goodnight." *Nuts—how much of that did they hear?* She headed up the stairs, mindful of the squeaky step halfway up. So much for "just friends" and "going slow." She unlocked her door and flicked on a light so she wouldn't trip and break her neck. The guys had placed the furniture and hung the curtains and drapes. The rest of the disaster was on her. The Tylers downstairs had offered to help carry anything she wanted to store in her section of the basement. If she ever finished unpacking, the place would be cute and cozy. Right now, though? A single path wound through the apartment. Sorta. And acute embarrassment was a good incentive to go slow. No way was she inviting a guy—any guy, no matter how comfortable—over to this mess.

Boxes and bins were sorted by contents. More or less. An uncomfortable number of containers were marked miscellaneous—probably where most of the stuff she couldn't find was lurking.

A breeze stirred the curtains and she shivered. She lowered the sash and pulled the drapes shut. The lights were still aglow at The Clowder. *Probably feeding the cats.*

She hadn't felt cold sitting outside with Brad. She'd been warm and comfortable, and she wanted to kiss him, so she did. Sort of. And now they were going out on Tuesday.

I need something fun to wear—nothing too dressy for the diner, but enough to show I care. Maybe the green sweater with the fall leaves?

She picked her way through the maze to her bedroom. The sweater was right there…in one of those boxes marked clothes. Or maybe in a suitcase? Sorting through extra clothing wasn't a priority. Mom and Dad's wedding photo and Grandma's afghan were much more important.

Until now. *I should swallow my pride and enlist Elsie's help. Good thing I have until Tuesday to figure out an outfit.*

****

Sure enough, a motor revved to life at Are You Kidding Me? o'clock in the morning. Maggie flopped back onto her pillows. A couple more hours sleep before work would be nice, but so would clearing the mess of boxes sometime before Christmas. And she kinda wanted to check the local noise ordinances. Most communities understood folks liked to sleep in on Sunday.

Oh, goodie…Cuthbert and a few of his closest friends were getting in on the act. Groaning, she slid out of bed and navigated by the thin sliver of sunlight stabbing through the chink in her drapes—and walked right into the corner of a carton. "Ouch—crud!" She hopped around on one foot. "Ow ow ow!" *Why does a stupid stubbed toe always feel like an amputation?*

Well, I'm awake now. She pulled sweats over her nightshirt and bundled her hair up with a scrunchie. If she was going to unpack for a bit, she could clean up later. Overhead, floorboards creaked and downstairs, the front door opened and shut. *Butch must be home from work, and the Tylers just left for their shop.*

Finding an outfit to go somewhere with Brad wasn't a horrible drag like preparing for one of Jack's fancy events—even if locating her favorite sweater did entail more actual work in this instance.

Brad was...comfortable. Sure, what she felt wasn't the glamourous fairy tale rush of love...or something...at first sight, but she liked being around him. She didn't feel like she had to look and act perfect every moment they were together. Kind of like how she felt around Ted, except she never wanted to kiss him.

Ew. No. Brain bleach, please. Or coffee.

Definitely coffee. The first glorious cup of the day was assembled and ready for consumption when her buzzer emitted a truly obnoxious noise. She wandered to the door and hit the talk button.

"Good morning, dear. It's Elsie. May I come up?"

Elsie. Right. She'd already seen the mess, and she wouldn't blink at sweats and messy hair. "Sure. I even have coffee." She opened the door and saw Elsie coming up the stairs with a covered dish in her hands.

"You're up early."

"Ezra—that is, Chief Parker—gave me a lift. Seems he got a bunch of calls about noise violations. Also vandalism possibly caused by a large dog—decorations knocked over, flowers dug up, a vintage birdbath broken—"

"Poo?" Maggie guessed.

"Poo. He'll take statements and then likely go have another chat with Mr. Carson."

"So you have a little time?"

"Of course, dear. What do you need?" Elsie moved around the kitchen, pouring herself a cup of coffee and loading up a dish for Maggie.

"I wondered…" She glanced around at the stacks of boxes. "That is, would you mind—"

Elsie came out and handed her a bowl and spoon. "Helping you unpack some of this?"

"Yes, thank you."

"Of course, dear. Anything in particular?"

Maggie scuffed the toe of her sneaker against the faded linoleum. Heat crept up the back of her neck. "If we could sort my clothes, that would be amazing."

Elsie laughed merrily. "I thought as much. Eat your food while it's warm."

Maggie didn't need to be told twice. Cheese, onions, and bacon exploded across her tastebuds. *"Mmmmffff."*

"You're welcome. Where would you like to start?" Elsie picked up Mom and Dad's wedding portrait from the top of a stack of boxes. "You have her smile. You'll want a very special place for this." She set the picture back, adjusting the stand carefully, and looked around the room. "That bay window will be lovely for the holidays."

Maggie gulped her mouthful of deliciousness and licked a few crumbs from her lips. "I want a big tree. I don't care if there's needles on the rug, or the ornaments don't match."

"They're the best kind." Elsie wandered over to the bedroom and stood in the doorway with her hands on her hips, surveying the chaos. "So, clothes?" She opened a box and scooped out an armload of garments.

"Yeah. I'm tired of cycling through the same two T-shirts on my days off. And…I'm going out Tuesday."

She paused, chewing her lip. "With Brad. Is that…okay?"

Elsie looked up from the sweaters she was refolding. "I'm not his mother, or yours. And anyway, you're both grown adults. I have no say in the matter." She graced Maggie with a smile that felt like a warm hug. "But if I did…yes, it's very okay."

****

"Okay—I can't take it anymore. What the heck are you so cheerful about?" Ted grumbled.

"Our shift is almost over, and I'm off tomorrow. Why shouldn't I be cheerful?" Maggie replied.

"Don't say that too loud—the universe might hear." He shut the equipment case he'd been restocking, crossed his arms, and leaned against the wall. "And it's been going on since Sunday." He freed one hand to tick things off on his fingers. "You didn't bat an eye when we had to scrub the entire kitchen after whatever Kelsey tried to make for lunch yesterday. You handed Matt the mop instead of beating him over the head with it when he tracked muddy boot prints all over the floor we'd just finished cleaning. Come on—spill—what do you have planned?"

"You know, I did just move. I have an apartment full of boxes to deal with."

"You just moved, and there's a single neighbor across the street. I bet he'd be happy to help you with all those boxes."

"What are you, twelve?"

Ted recrossed his arms and slouched a little more diligently against the wall. "I'm observant."

Maggie snorted.

Ted raised an eyebrow. "Dude spends half his day

scooping cat boxes. I'm betting that little show of grace and deportment won't put him off."

"Fine. I have plans. Happy?"

"Plans with Brad?"

"Why do you care?"

"Because you're my partner. Also I've got twenty bucks riding on it."

"Wait—who the hell are you betting with about my love life or lack thereof?"

"His sister."

Chapter Eight

Brad checked his appearance in the mirror. "What do you think, Mocha?"

Mocha blinked open his huge blue eyes and stretched luxuriously. He head-butted Brad and rubbed against his hip, demanding pets. Brad chuckled and stroked his long, soft brown fur. "Yes, you're very handsome, but what about me?" Mocha turned in a tight circle, snuggled into the comforter, and ignored the question. Nixie batted something around under the bed—hopefully one of the five hundred or so actual cat toys littering the house. He glanced around the cluttered room but didn't notice anything out of place. Well, books were escaping onto the floor, but there was nothing unusual about that.

I'm neat, clean, and presentable. It'll have to do.

He clattered from his attic bedroom, nearly taking the express route when Nixie dodged between his feet with a pencil in her mouth.

"Whoa." Hollyn shut April's door with a soft click. "Pants without holes, shoes, and a shirt with a collar? What's the occasion? You didn't forget to tell me reporters are coming again, did you?" She waved a hand vaguely at her rumpled purple and black cat-print scrubs.

"That was once, Hollyn. Once."

Her eyes widened, as did her grin. "Do you have a date?"

"I'm going to the diner."

She crossed her arms and slouched against the wall. "Uh-huh. You never leave the house voluntarily. You order food online, then forget and jump three feet in the air when the doorbell rings."

"And today, I'm going to the diner."

"By yourself?"

He sighed. "With Maggie. There. Are you happy now?"

"Very. Don't screw it up."

****

Maggie took a long sip of her root beer float, then sighed in satisfaction. Brad grinned at her across the chipped tabletop. She settled into the creaky maroon vinyl of the booth and grinned right back.

"What can I tell you? I'm a simple girl. When I'm hungry, I want to eat, and I want to be able to recognize what's on my plate." *Food. Actual food, none of that micro-gastro-fusion stuff.*

"Something we have in common."

She tilted her head slightly. "You seem pretty relaxed today."

"Well, I'm in good company." Laugh lines crinkled the corners of his mouth. "And I turned in a big project yesterday."

"What about?" Maggie took another slurp and leaned forward.

"African animals."

"That sounds interesting."

"Yeah, it is." Brad looked as if he wanted to say more, but he reached for his milkshake instead. A slight crease appeared on his forehead.

Millie bustled over in her familiar frowzy pink plaid

uniform with a pen tucked behind her ear. "How are you folks doing today? Everything good?"

"Great, thank you, Millie."

"Perfect," Maggie added.

Millie eyed them expectantly. "I heard the county surveyor's paying a visit to your street."

"Um…yeah. That old feud between the Carsons and the Morgans about the property line. They've been wrangling since we were kids."

"Is that the house with the gazillion gnomes and flamingos along the side yard?" Maggie asked.

Brad nodded. "Yup. The side facing Mr. Carson. Wait 'til they put up the holiday lights."

Millie added an affirmative *hmmph*. "Someday that old crank is gonna need help, and he'll wonder why no one wants anything to do with him." She *hmmph*'d again, then grinned at them. "Well, let me know if you need anything. We're running a special on deluxe banana splits today—the perfect size for sharing."

The tips of Brad's ears flamed bright red, and he pushed his food around the plate with his fork. "Um…thanks. We'll let you know."

Millie finally took the hint and wandered over to the front register. She and Gail had their heads together whispering.

It won't be long before all of Main Street knows we were here together again. So much for privacy in a small town.

"Brad?" Maggie touched his arm. "Hey, did I say something wrong? Your project—it really does sound interesting."

He shook his head slightly. "I'm sorry. It's my fault. This is the part of the conversation where the other person usually asks if I'm writing kid's books until I 'sell my novel.' "

"You're writing a novel, too? When do you have time?"

He huffed out a humorless little laugh. "I'm not. I really like what I write, but a lot of people seem to think the only acceptable topics for male authors are spies and detectives."

She studied him. "Actually, I could see you writing something like James Herriot or maybe Cleveland Amory."

"They were two of my mom's favorites, and Elsie's, too."

"And for the record? I'm not most people." She picked the lettuce off her club sandwich, smooshed the layers together and took a bite.

"No, you're not. I apologize."

She chewed and swallowed. "Apology accepted."

"Anyway, this last project makes me want to go to the zoo."

"That sounds like fun." *Oops. I didn't mean to invite myself. Really.* "I mean, I haven't been in ages." Jack was always "too busy" for such things. But heaven forfend she miss one of his stuffy cocktail parties or networking events. She returned her attention to the much nicer guy in front of her.

"Well, I have a little break before the next round of projects, so I want to spend at least one day doing something fun."

"What else will you do with your break?"

He paused slightly in his methodical consumption of meatloaf and mashed potatoes. "I want to try and trap some cats from the woods."

"Kittens?"

"No. We're mostly past kitten season for the year. I hope."

"Wait—there's an actual season?"

He nodded, chewing and swallowing. "Places with a cold season, like our area, usually have a bit of a break over the winter when there's not as much food available. The idea is to trap as many adults as possible and have them spayed or neutered, so there are fewer kittens next spring."

"And will you try to find them adopters?"

"It depends. Adults aren't always ready for life indoors. But if we can neuter and vaccinate them, that's something. We also have connections with people who place barn cats."

"That's pretty amazing."

Brad smiled, then glanced at his ever-so-interesting plate before meeting her eyes again. "So…would you like to go to the zoo with me?"

"I would, but…" She huffed out a breath. "Look…I'm not good at this relationship…stuff."

He shrugged. "Neither am I, really, but I enjoy your company, and…I thought the zoo might be a fun thing to do together. Okay?"

She chewed her lip uncertainly. "The thing is…look, I'm just going to say this, all right?"

Brad nodded.

"I worked incredibly hard to be certified for my job. I'm a good paramedic, and I really love helping people. But it's not the sort of job that shuts off at five o'clock on Friday. I guess…if we're gonna do this…I need you to understand that."

"I know it's not exactly the same, but I watched my

sister work for years to get the career she wanted. A career that has resulted in more early mornings, late nights, and disrupted holidays than I can count. I'm willing to give this a shot if you are."

After a long moment, she smiled and extended her hand across the table. "Deal?"

"Deal." He shook her hand firmly.

Chapter Nine

It was a great day for a drive. The leaves were starting to turn, adding pops of brilliant color to the landscape. Lots of families had already set up for Halloween. Purple or orange lights outlined eaves and porches. It was too early—and too warm—for carved pumpkins, but some lawns sported decorations ranging from light up plastic ghosts to terrifyingly detailed scenes straight out of a horror movie.

Unfortunately, something else caught Brad's attention. "What the hell is he doing?"

The school bus in front of them swerved, even though the road was dry. Brad eased off the gas.

Maggie clutched her armrest. "Brad? What's he doing?"

"I don't know, but the road becomes windy around the golf course." He vaguely noticed Maggie grabbing her cell phone. Then he stomped on the brakes as the bus veered off the road and through a chain-link fence, scattering a flock of Canada geese before stopping in the middle of the golf course.

"Pull over."

Brad flicked on his hazards and pulled to the side of the road.

Maggie jabbed a contact on her phone. "Come on you guys—pick up—pick up. Ted? It's Maggie—shut up about my day off—we're on Route 3. A school bus full of kids just went off the road. You heard me. Right through the fence and onto the golf course. Send some help out here. Look for the red SUV with the hazards on."

She hung up and turned to Brad. "I need to assess the situation. Stay in the car."

"I'm first-aid certified, and I have a pretty good kit in the trunk."

She paused with her door halfway open. "Your certification is current?"

Brad nodded.

"Okay. Can you follow my instructions precisely?"

Another terse nod.

"Show me your kit."

Brad ran around to the back of the car and grabbed the gym bag he used for a first-aid kit.

She unzipped the bag and examined the contents. "Wow. This is great."

Brad shrugged as he shouldered the bag. "We spend a lot of time in the woods looking for cats. Stuff happens. This seemed like a wise investment."

"Good thinking. Now follow my lead. Remember, you're a civilian."

"Yes, ma'am."

They moved carefully through the damaged fence and onto the golf course. Fortunately, the bus had come to a safe stop—upright and not in the pond. The current crop of geese was ticked off by the intrusion, but the bus was large and loud enough to be perceived as a predator, so they'd retreated to the far side of the green.

The driver bent over with his hands on his knees, wheezing, even as he directed the kids off the bus, trying to count heads as they passed.

Maggie hurried over and steadied him. "Sir? Sir are you okay?"

He nodded and tried to catch his breath. "Some darn fool dog was chasing a rabbit. Big feller—one of them firehouse dogs. I didn't want to hit him if I could help it."

She shot Brad a look—they both had an excellent idea of what local canine might be described as a "firehouse dog."

"Not your fault, sir. Look, I need to ask—the police will have to test you for alcohol—"

"Not a drop."

Maggie smiled reassuringly. "I didn't think so, but it's procedure."

"I don't drink a beer at the Sunday ball game—I'm that careful." The old man shook his head. "Thirty years perfect driving record blown to hell by someone's darn dog."

"Let's not worry about that right now. How are you feeling?"

"Like I got an elephant stood on my chest."

"Okay." She took a firmer grip on his arm. Brad took the other. "How many kids on board?"

"Eighteen." He tried to straighten, one hand pressed to his chest. "Janice, do you have your brother's inhaler?"

A girl with glasses and dark, serious eyes nodded. She had a smaller boy firmly by the hand.

"Good girl," he wheezed. "Go sit under the big oak tree."

"Brad, get them away from the bus and take a head count." Maggie tightened her grip on the bus driver.

"Will do. You got him?" Maggie nodded and he

stepped away.

Brad hauled himself up into the bus. "Okay, kids—"

"Hey—you're the Cat Guy!"

"Yes, I am. And right now, I need you to listen, okay? I need you to come and follow me. We're gonna go sit under the big oak tree over there and wait for the fire department. Come on now."

Maggie spared him a smile, even as she checked the driver's pulse. The kids were shaken up, but delighted to spend time with the Cat Guy. "Go keep an eye on them. Check for injuries."

"I will." He hopped down from the bus and squeezed Maggie's arm.

The kids who'd gotten off the bus were sitting in a circle under the tree, evidently under the big sister's direction.

"Good job," Brad complimented her. "Which one is your brother?"

She pointed to a little boy seated right next to her.

He crouched to the child's level. "Hey, buddy, I hear you use an inhaler sometimes."

The boy nodded.

"Do you feel like you need it now?"

Headshake.

"You feel okay otherwise?"

"Yeah. Is the lady really a fireman?"

"She's a paramedic, but yes, she works for the fire department."

"She's pretty. Is she your girlfriend?"

Heat crept up the back of Brad's neck. "She's my new neighbor. You guys sit tight, okay? I'm gonna check on your friends."

****

The on-duty ambulance crew shooed Maggie away from the bus, and she crossed the grass to where Brad and the kids sat under a tree. The children were enraptured by whatever he was telling them. He was always good-looking, but there was just something about the way his eyes lit up when he smiled at his young audience. He was doing an admirable job of distracting them from the sirens and accompanying chaos.

"Hey, what's going on over here?" She sank to the grass beside him.

"We're talking about animals. Which one's your favorite?"

She pretended to consider the question. "Wow. I can only choose one? What's the one that looks like a ferret but stands up straight?"

"Meerkat." several young voices yelled.

"Yup. Meerkats. I like them."

"So do I," Brad replied. "So…who likes elephants?"

There was a chorus of happy shrieks, but before Brad could say anything else, a firefighter wearing a white captain's helmet approached the group. Maggie scrambled to her feet.

"I hate to break this up, but the principal is here with a bus to collect these youngsters. School nurse, too. Is there anything she needs to know?"

"Just a few bumps and bruises," Brad replied, standing. "I think they're more shook up than anything else."

They waved as the principal shepherded the children off to the waiting bus.

"We were lucky," Brad observed. "How's the driver?"

"Pretty shaken up. We're taking him in for observation. He's a bit old for this kind of shock. Lucky for him, he was able to stop the bus more or less safely, and you two were here. Thank you for your assistance, Mr. MacKenzie. I know how to reach you if I have any questions."

Brad grinned. "How's your son doing with Spot?"

"He adores that cat. He's saving his allowance for a fancy cat tree he found online."

"That's great. He's always welcome at The Clowder if he needs more community service hours."

Maggie admired Brad's easy manner with her boss…to the point she almost missed his next words.

"Maggie, isn't this supposed to be your day off?"

"Yes, sir."

"Well then, suppose you get back to whatever you were doing when this mess started? I understand you were in the same vehicle, so could you type up a brief account of the incident and email it to my office, cc'd to Chief Parker?"

"Will do, sir."

The captain headed onto the green to supervise his men, and Brad and Maggie walked to his car. Neither noticed a reporter snapping photographs.

Chapter Ten

"Well, that was a bit more excitement than I expected," Brad joked as they climbed into the car.

"Story of my life. Move to a nice quiet neighborhood in the suburbs so I can get some rest…"

"Well, in defense of Carson Circle, this particular adventure happened halfway across town."

"Look, you were—"

"I just wanted to say—" They both spoke at the same time.

"Ladies first." Brad grinned and tried to maintain his focus on the road. Maggie was a powerful distraction.

"You were great with those kids."

"Well, I've written a lot of books, so I have a range of topics and suitable language at my disposal. I'm glad I could be helpful."

"And what were you going to say?"

"I thought you were pretty amazing. I mean…I know exploding vehicles is a thing that happens in movies, not real life, but it's still kinda hard to shake the idea. Part of me would have been much happier if you'd come with me and the kids, but you were so calm and confident it was easy to follow your lead.…you believed everything would be okay, so I believed it, too."

Maggie shrugged slightly, her cheeks blushing a wonderful rosy pink. "It's my job."

"You're really good at it."

"Thank you." She paused a moment. "I'm glad you were with me. If I was alone, I'd have had to decide between leaving the kids unsupervised or taking care of the driver."

"I don't know what I would do in that situation."

"I don't think anyone does until they're in the middle of it. But I had you, so I didn't have to make that call. Thanks for listening to me."

"Why wouldn't I listen to a professional first responder in an emergency?"

"You're a very enlightened fellow, but trust me, sexism is alive and well. I think we made a pretty good team."

"We sure did." He turned into their street. "Do you want to use my computer to write your report?"

"Good idea. We can both look it over…and we should probably include a scan of your first-aid card."

"I'll set you up at my desk." Brad pulled into his driveway, drained as the rush of adrenaline receded.

"Did you use anything from your kit? When's the last time you did an inventory?"

"Just a couple of bandages and wipes, but restocking is probably not a bad idea." He walked to the rear of the vehicle and hoisted the bag over his shoulder.

Elsie burst out the front door and bustled over to hug them both. "Are you two okay? You were on the news."

"There were reporters?" Brad asked.

"The local cable news picked up the story," Elsie explained. " 'Local author and off-duty paramedic save kids.' And of course, people recognized you, so The Clowder's social media is blowing up."

"Of course it is." Brad sighed and rubbed the back of his neck. "Could you do a 'Brad was happy to help, but please try to keep to the topic' sort of post?"

Elsie set her hands on her hips. "What do you think I've been doing?"

"Thanks…really. See you tomorrow?"

"Of course you will."

They both waved as Elsie climbed into her car and pulled away, then Brad led the way inside, scooping up Nixie before she could bolt out the door. He and Se snoozed in their cat tree and didn't even twitch a whisker.

****

Maggie followed him through the entryway into the living room. Overstuffed bookshelves lined the walls, and a comfy-looking sectional couch strewn with autumn-themed throw pillows faced a flat-screen TV. A repurposed dining table housing an array of computer equipment dominated the room, along with an ergonomic office chair containing an enormous, extremely floofy cat.

She smiled delightedly and reached out to see if the cat was as cuddly as he looked.

"Mocha, get down," Brad instructed.

The magnificent fluffy creature blinked brilliant sapphire eyes at the two humans, then pointedly laid his head on his paws and feigned sleep.

"That's…not an alley cat." Maggie stroked Mocha's soft fur with an enchanted smile.

"No, he's not. That's Mocha. He's a chocolate point bicolor mink Ragdoll cat."

She blinked. "That's a mouthful."

"That's the description on the one and only photo I found online that looks like him."

"He looks like a fancy show cat."

"Well, he's certainly a diva. At least once I got him cleaned up. I found him in the woods. He was filthy, matted, and starving. He did not appreciate the bath and shave."

"You shaved him?" Her eyes widened in horror.

"Mats, burrs, and did I mention filthy? Obviously, his magnificent floof grew back."

"How'd he get out there?"

"No clue. He wasn't wearing a collar, and he doesn't have a chip or tattoo. We never found a lost pet report matching his description. He'd been declawed—and don't get me started on that—so there was no way he was going back outside. Plus, he's pretty clueless."

She crouched beside the chair to take a better look. "Well, I think he's gorgeous."

Mocha lifted his head and gave a slow blink as though agreeing with her.

Brad shook his head in fond exasperation and hefted the fluffy monstrosity in his arms. "Come on, buddy. Maggie needs the chair. You can snooze on the sofa."

Mocha whined but was happy enough to curl up in the couch cushions.

"There's lint roller around here…somewhere…"

Maggie chuckled and swiped half-heartedly at the seat of the chair a few times before sitting. After their little side quest, her outfit was destined for the hamper. At least she hadn't snagged her sweater.

"Use my laptop." He slid his hands under the clear glass riser protecting the keyboard and switched from The Clowder's live stream to a blank document.

"This is amazing."

Two flat-screen monitors took up most of the table. Each screen was divided to show four different views of the house. She recognized the upstairs cat rooms and the front porch.

"I can monitor the whole house from here and choose which cam is live on the internet."

Maggie studied the images. "Do you ever use all the rooms?"

"Oh, yeah. Spring and summer, we tend to have a full house. All three cat rooms, the isolation room, playpens in the dining room and Hollyn's room, and sometimes cats even take over the guest room. Luckily, we get a break over the winter."

"And what do you do then?"

"Clean *everything*."

"Sounds like a slow day at the firehouse." She tapped the screen with her fingertip. "Why's this room so bare?"

"That's the isolation room. We like to keep the newcomers in there for a day or two. We put just the necessities in there, so there's less to scrub down. We also use that room if we discover a case of ringworm."

"Good thinking."

"Some lessons only have to be learned once." He shuddered at the memory. "Anyway...I'm going to throw in a load of wash, then check on the upstairs residents. Um...printer's over there, and feel free to help yourself to anything in the kitchen that looks fit for human consumption."

"I'll tell Elsie you said that."

"Okay, okay...just avoid the takeout containers. And I guess...yell if you need anything."

"I will."

****

Typing up the report didn't take too long. She read

the document and hit save. Then she glanced at the monitor and saw Brad upstairs in April's room, checking on the kittens. A sticky note on the monitor said April was on the live stream today. Cosmos and Nebula frolicked happily in their room. *I could play with them for a little while.*

That wasn't weird, right? She'd been invited often enough by Brad, Elsie, and Hollyn. She slipped upstairs and saw Brad through the glass in April's door. He sat on the floor with three tiny kittens using him for a jungle gym. His expression was open and unguarded, and his smiles at the kittens' antics were genuine. He was attractive by any standard, but the joy and kindness he radiated when working with the cats really tugged at her heartstrings. No matter how hard she tried to resist. *Loves animals, does his own laundry, and knows how to make coffee. You could do worse.*

She waved to catch his attention, then gestured to the other room. He nodded and gave her a thumbs up. A kitten promptly launched itself at his thumb and attacked with all the ferocity a four-week-old ball of fluff could manage.

And okay...maybe this wasn't quite how she pictured a first date, but up until the runaway school bus, it had been a pretty good afternoon. Good enough to make her wonder what a day with no interference from either of their jobs might be like.

Chapter Eleven

Thursday morning, Brad stood on the porch, signing for a delivery when a police car pulled up in front of Maggie's place. She swung her legs out of the car and stood slowly, weariness etched in every movement. Her face was pale with dark smudges under her eyes. She wore a set of plain gray sweats, and her hair hung in damp tangles. She looked...small, somehow, and vulnerable. Brad pushed the clipboard into the delivery guy's hands and jogged across the street, leaving the boxes piled haphazardly on the front steps.

"Maggie? Are you okay? Where's your car?"

"I'm fine."

"You're not," Chief Parker responded. The laugh lines around his mouth were sunken in today. He turned his attention to Brad. "Her car is parked at the county firehouse, where it is perfectly safe and where it will remain for at least the next twenty-four hours."

"What happened?"

The chief sighed and seemed to age before his eyes. "There was a bad fire at the old paint factory." He paused, looking down at the pavement before focusing on Brad. "Real bad."

"That place is creepy as hell. I went there last year with animal control to help trap a colony of strays that had moved in. I'm surprised the building's still standing." He shuddered, recalling crumbling brickwork, rusting iron beams, and rotting floorboards. He'd spent a solid thirty minutes in the shower scrubbing the filth off his skin. In the end, the dank smell permeated his clothing so strongly he'd just tossed everything.

"It's not anymore." The chief glanced up at the third floor windows of the Adams place. "Butch…didn't make it."

Brad edged closer to Maggie and reached for her.

"I'm fine." She tried to sidestep him.

"No one who was there is fine, Maggie." Chief Parker touched her arm. "You should know that better than most."

Brad frowned. "I don't think you should be alone right now."

"She shouldn't."

"Look, why don't you come over to my place?"

Maggie mustered a tired smile. "I'm not very good company today."

"You don't have to talk to anyone if you don't want to. Well, except Elsie's gonna feed you. But seriously, we have a guest room, or you can hole up in one of the kitten rooms. Just…don't be by yourself right now, okay?"

The chief forced a grin and shoved his hat farther back on his head. "Kittens and Elsie Tatum's cooking? If my shift hadn't just started, I'd take you up on that offer myself."

Brad held out a hand to Maggie and dropped his voice to a tone usually reserved for skittish kitties. "I'm pretty sure Elsie's watching from the window, so if I come home without you, she's gonna march across the street and bang on your door. So why don't you save us all the trouble and come home with me?"

She still looked rebellious, so the chief spoke up again. "Look, Maggie…I've been in this line of work a lot longer than you. I know you think you need to be tough about these things, but what happened last night ain't about being tough. The incident was bad enough the state is sending a trauma counselor to speak to the first responders."

Brad blanched at that bit of information and edged closer to Maggie.

"What do you expect me to do?"

"I expect you to go be with your friends. Get some rest and food and cuddle the kittens. And if you need to cry, you go right ahead. I promise you; no one will think the less of you."

All the fight drained out of Maggie at once. She took Brad's hand and let him pull her in close.

Elsie appeared at Brad's front door with Nixie tucked firmly under her arm. "Breakfast! Will you be joining us, Chief Parker?"

He tipped his hat with a cordial smile. "Not today, I'm afraid, but I thank you for the invitation."

"And do you have anything packed for your lunch?"

"Well—"

"I thought as much." She held up a brown paper bag.

With a sheepish grin, the chief ambled across the street and collected his lunch.

Brad had never wanted to hug anyone as much as he wanted to hug Maggie just then, but when he half-raised his arm, telegraphing his intention, she stiffened under his touch, clinging to her professional façade like a lifeline. He allowed her that bit of distance as they crossed the street and walked up his front steps. Elsie, of course, had no such compunction. She engulfed Maggie in a fierce one-armed embrace, squishing Nixie between them.

"Come on in, dear. There's a French onion strata, fresh from the oven, and bacon. Lots and lots of bacon."

Maggie's lips curled in the faintest shadow of a smile. "Bacon isn't a universal cure-all, Elsie."

Brad cracked a grin at her words.

"It'll do quite nicely until one comes along." She waved Maggie to a seat at the island and shooed He and Se out from under her feet. "Coffee? Or have you had too much already?" She passed a travel mug to Chief Parker, who tipped his hat again and sidled out of the kitchen.

"Way too much."

Brad quirked an eyebrow. "How do you know…?"

"Some of us pay attention to the news, Brad. Why don't you make Maggie a hot chocolate?"

"Oh, I don't want to be any trouble—"

"Nonsense, dear. Friends look after one another. Were you hurt?"

"No. I was doing triage in the parking lot."

Elsie slid a loaded plate in front of Maggie. Brad snitched a piece of bacon from the serving plate, and she swatted his arm.

"Make Maggie's hot chocolate, then finish bringing in the delivery."

"Yes, ma'am." He fiddled with dials on the coffee machine. It hissed and spit and eventually produced a steaming cup of fragrant chocolate. Brad added a pouf of whipped cream and handed Maggie a mug shaped like a silly cat face. "Feel free to go anywhere in the house. Really."

She favored him with a thin smile. "Thanks."

"After Maggie eats, she can come with me on my rounds. I'll show her where everything is."

"Okay, then. I'll take care of those boxes." He wanted to say more but was unsure what…and much as he loved Elsie, he didn't really want an audience. So he settled for squeezing Maggie's arm gently.

****

Maggie ate mechanically. Anything Elsie cooked was delicious, but her mouth was so dry nothing had any taste.

"Do you want a distraction, or do you need to just curl up and sleep?"

"I don't know."

"That's perfectly natural, dear."

"I don't want to—" She promptly shut up when Elsie whirled around and pointed a spatula at her.

"You are not a bother, and you're not in the way." She slipped the pan of food into the warm oven, hung up the black cat oven mitt, and washed her hands. "Come along if you're done eating."

Maggie obediently slid off the stool and set her empty dishes in the sink. She followed Elsie to the front hall, where Brad sorted boxes.

He tossed Maggie a small jingling parcel. "I bet there's something in there Nebula and Cosmos would like."

"There's food warming in the oven," Elsie told him. "Make sure you eat something." She led the way upstairs. "I know Brad started to give you the grand tour the other day—"

"But mayhem happened."

"That's pretty common around here. Anyway…that end of the hall is Hollyn's room, the guest room, and the

94

people bathroom. This end is April's litter, Nebula and Cosmos, the linen closet, one currently empty cat room, and the cat bathroom."

That penetrated Maggie's haze of exhaustion. "Don't tell me he has them toilet trained."

Elsie laughed merrily. "Nope. Not even the ones who live here. We just try to keep the other bathroom for the human residents and use this one for the cats or cat-related messes."

"This is an amazing setup."

"It is. Their mother would be so proud of what they've accomplished. Planning, designing, and renovating the house took a lot of hard—" Elsie cut off midsentence as she spotted something on the floor. "Brad MacKenzie, was this a basket of clean laundry before Mocha got into it?"

At the sound of his name, Mocha blinked one eye open, then curled into a tighter ball and pretended to go to sleep.

Maggie winced. Elsie's voice could easily carry across a crowded schoolyard.

"Um…yes," came Brad's sheepish reply.

"And would you like me to fold everything and put it away?"

"Yes…please."

Elsie grinned at Maggie. "I would have done it anyway, but sometimes I like to remind him not to take people for granted. Only the cat laundry, mind you. He's entirely on his own otherwise."

"Can I help?"

"No, thank you, dear. Why don't you go in and play with Cosmos and Nebula?" Elsie checked the notes on the doors. "They're not live right now. Brad scooped their box and fed them already, but there's a packet of treats in the cabinet if they beg too much." She squeezed Maggie's arm briefly. "Take all the time you need. And remember…kittens are very absorbent." She turned her attention back to the laundry basket and flapped her hand at the occupant. "Now, you, just shoo."

Maggie stepped out of her shoes and slipped inside. Cosmos and Nebula stared at her curiously while she settled cross-legged on the floor. The package Brad handed her jingled and both kitties bounded over to investigate. Cosmos patted her leg as if to say, "Hurry up, lady."

Maggie opened the parcel curiously. Someone who watched The Clowder's live streams sent a package of little felt catnip mice and another of balls with tiny bells inside. A note and a check fluttered out. Of course, it wasn't really her business…and Maggie knew she should put them aside for Brad, but she was curious.

Dear Clowder Folks,

I'm writing this on behalf of my mom. She was really depressed when she moved to a nursing home and couldn't keep her cat anymore. But don't worry—Lillibet lives with us now. I bring my laptop when I visit, and she loves watching your videos. I can't tell you how much they brighten her day. I found her a plush toy that looks just like Mocha, and she cuddles him all the time.

Anyway…Mom picked some toys for the kitties, and I'm enclosing a check for food or whatever you might need. Thanks so much for all your hard work. You do more good than you'll ever realize.

Nebula grabbed the packet of mice and tried to chew through the cellophane. Maggie laughed and reclaimed the package. She set the letter and check aside carefully.

Then she tore open the package and offered a mousie to Nebula, who grabbed the toy and sniffed ecstatically.

Meanwhile, Cosmos crept next to her and meowed softly. Maggie fished out another mouse and offered it to him, but Nebula reached out a lighting swift paw and snatched the second toy. Her brother eyed her with a look of extreme betrayal.

Maggie laughed and took the third mouse from the package and aimed for Cosmos again. Nebula grabbed that one as well.

"Hey—that's not nice."

Nebula was entirely unrepentant with a toy in each paw and one in her mouth.

"This one's for Cosmos. I mean it."

Nebula had other ideas. She somehow managed to stuff one of the toys she already had underneath herself and grab the fourth one from Maggie's hand. Maggie blinked. Cosmos blinked. Nebula looked smug. Even by cat standards.

Laughing, Maggie grabbed her phone and snapped a picture for Brad. Cosmos meowed indignantly and patted Maggie's sleeve for attention.

"Okay. Yes, I know…your sister's being a jerk. How about these?" She shook the package of jingle balls enticingly. Of course, this package didn't tear easily. The plastic finally split with a sharp tug, sending balls rolling across the floor. Cosmos immediately pounced, batting balls all over the room gleefully. Nebula looked from her pile of mousies to the balls. Then back again. Finally, she scampered off after her brother.

Maggie laughed until tears ran down her cheeks. And yes, maybe there was a slight edge of hysteria too, but the release felt good, all the same.

Brad tapped lightly on the glass, then stepped inside the room. He rubbed the back of his neck. "Um…hi. My sister is home and has informed me in no uncertain terms that I'm a horse's…er…you know."

Maggie swiped at her eyes while Cosmos and Nebula deserted her to swarm up Brad's legs. *Good thing he's wearing jeans.* "Any particular reason, or is that the way you two express sibling affection?"

"In this case, mostly for leaving you alone with these hooligans. I'm not entirely sure what I should have done instead, and she refuses to tell me, so could you give me a hint?"

"I'm fine. These two are great company."

Brad winced as their claws dug through his pant leg. He unhooked Cosmos before those claws sunk into body parts he probably preferred unpunctured. "Um…I think I've mentioned, I'm not very good at this."

"Me, neither. I'm fine, really." She sniffled a bit. "I'm used to being on my own." *Even when I was with Jack. Maybe especially then.*

"But you shouldn't be. At least…not now. Come on downstairs? No one will bother you if you really want some space, but the couch is awfully comfy, and Mocha's always in the market for a cuddle."

"Well, I am getting a bit stiff on the floor."

Brad offered her a hand, and she let him pull her to her feet.

"I'm really glad you're okay."

He extended his arms awkwardly as if unsure of his reception. Maggie tried to smile but suspected it turned out to be more of a weird grimace. She stepped forward and let him pull her into a tight hug. His touch was warm and steady—not demanding anything—just holding her safe.

"Last night was really awful," she mumbled into his shirt front. "The injuries were horrible…no matter how much you train…when your friends are the ones who are hurt…" Her voice trailed off into a muffled sob. She straightened, putting a breath of space between them, and dabbed ineffectually at a wet spot on the front of his shirt. "Sorry. And Butch—I only met him a few times, but you were neighbors for years. Were you friends?"

"He was sort of a loner. I'm not sure if he was close to anyone. I guess Chief Parker knows or will by the end of the day." He rubbed her arms. "Hey…you're among friends here. You have absolutely nothing to be sorry about. If you're ready for a little company, Elsie would like to feed you again, and Mocha wants to introduce you to the joys of the big sofa."

"Mocha does, huh?"

"Mocha makes an excellent substitute teddy bear. Very comfy in winter. Summer? Not so much. Not that it deters him."

****

Mocha did, in fact, make an excellent teddy bear. He was still wrapped around Maggie when she woke, slightly disoriented on the comfy sofa. She vaguely recalled Brad draping a couple of warm throw blankets over her. And…had he pressed a gentle kiss to her forehead? Or had she dreamed that bit?

She was cozy and secure here—almost more at home than in her own apartment. Strategically placed nightlights provided gentle illumination. She reached out blearily for her phone to check the time. It was on the coffee table with a key and a note. Curious, she used her phone as a makeshift flashlight.

Maggie,

Feel free to stay as long as you like. There's a guest room upstairs, or you can keep sharing Mocha's sofa. I'm leaving you a key in case you need to go back to your apartment for anything. I guess you're an official part of The Clowder now. But like I said...please stay as long as you need.

Brad

Mocha butted his head against Maggie's hand, looking for pets.

"What do you say, buddy? Think I can keep sharing your sofa for the rest of the night?"

Mocha just purred in response. Loudly.

Chapter Twelve

Brad glanced around at the freshly washed windows and floor of what used to be the family dining room. A faded photo of his mom smiled from among carefully framed cat artwork sent in by viewers and adopters. She would have loved what they'd done with the place. She'd have adored having a house full of kittens to spoil. She'd also have been delighted to finally box up all those fussy old dust collectors from Nana MacKenzie's house.

He placed the UV light fixture in the center of the room and switched it on. The unit needed to run for a few hours to disinfect the room. He checked his watch. Time to take a break from manual labor and work on the holiday PSAs. By the time he finished, the plastic playpen panels he'd set out in the backyard should be dry. He sat at his computer—and Cuthbert started barking his fool head off. Again. From the racket the usually unperturbable He and Se were making; he might even be inside the yard.

Brad stalked to the front window, shushing the two bristling tabbies gently. He twitched aside the curtains, and sure enough—Cuthbert was bouncing around the yard, knocking over the paper bags full of leaves.

"You're lucky I hauled the garden hose around to the back." It wasn't really the dog's fault, and he wouldn't *really* spritz him. Probably.

He shoved his feet into his shoes and headed

outside. "Go on, Cuthbert. Shoo! Go home."

He whistled for Cuthbert's attention, then lobbed a stick in the general direction of old man Carson's house. Cuthbert charged after the stick at full speed—right down the middle of the street. Brad shook his head. The Circle itself was pretty safe, but he'd suspected Cuthbert was wandering outside the neighborhood, even before the school bus incident. Someday the dog was going to run out of luck. He really didn't want to think about what might happen then.

He leaned the bags of leaves against the fence and looked around, scanning for any other damage—or deposits. He'd have to rake—again—before town hall received mysterious complaints about leaves.

Then he heard the faint mewing. He frowned, trying to pinpoint the source. The windows were shut, so he wasn't hearing the resident cats. He didn't have live traps set this close to the house. He and Hollyn had educated the neighbors into keeping their own cats safely indoors.

Brad kept his steps light and tried to tune out the whoosh of distant traffic and the crunch of crisp leaves. There—the grate at the end of the driveway. He hunkered down on his belly and used his phone for a flashlight, ignoring the chill from the pavement penetrating his clothes. The plaintive mewls grew louder. Finally, the wavering beam illuminated a bedraggled gray cat huddled in the storm drain.

"Okay, buddy. I'll get you out of there. I promise."

He heaved himself to his feet and ran for the garage. He grabbed a heavy-duty flashlight, prybar, and a small travel cage, then glanced around for anything else that might be useful. Another pair of hands could be helpful, but Hollyn was in her office today. He could go bang on

Maggie's door but…it was one thing to invite someone over to cuddle kittens and quite another to ask for help climbing into a mucky storm drain. Besides, it was entirely possible she was sleeping off one of those insanely long shifts. *Nope—I'm on my own.*

He stared at the iron grate covering the grungy storm drain. He scraped aside a layer of slimy old leaves with his foot and looked for a gap to slide the pry bar into. A rank smell drifted up from the grate. *Well, that's just gross.*

After a few minutes effort he was filthy and sweating and he'd barely managed to shift the grate a few inches. He straightened his aching back and scrubbed his forehead against his shirtsleeve. The miserable thing was heavy. *If I can just shove it aside…* One last heave and the grate shifted out of the slot with a horrible shriek of metal on concrete. He laid on his belly again and shone the light into the small space.

"Hey buddy…c'mere…I'll take you someplace warm and dry."

The noise unsettled the cat and he cowered at the far end of the drain—entirely too close to the mouth of a pipe for Brad's comfort. He extended his arm slowly. If the cat spooked and darted into the pipe— *No. Don't even think it.*

"C'mon, pal. I know Cuthbert scared you, but he's gone now. No doggos…I promise."

"Brad? What on earth are you doing?"

Maggie's voice startled him, and he banged his forehead on the rough concrete of the drain. The cat scuttled even farther away. *Don't swear, don't swear, don't swear…* "Hey, Maggie, can you please grab me a can of cat food from the house?"

"There's a cat in there?"

"Yeah. Cuthbert chased him in somehow. He's pretty scared, and I need something to lure him."

Maggie crouched and tried to peer around him. "You're bleeding."

"I'm fine," he assured her, still speaking in that measured voice. "But a can of food would be really helpful right now."

Maggie stood and jogged toward the house, returning promptly with an open can. "I brought the stinky tuna."

"Excellent choice." Brad snaked his arm out of the drain without taking his eyes off the cat.

"What else can I do?"

"Take one of those old towels and block off the other end of the pipe in case he scoots that way."

He stretched his arm into the drain, holding the can of food. He winced as he lost another layer of skin to the rough concrete. "Check this out, buddy. Tooooooona. C'mon...come get it."

"Would I fit in there? I'm thinner than you."

"My arms are longer, and it's pretty gross in here."

"That's why I borrowed your hoodie." She sat back on her heels and studied the situation. "What if we moved the grate? Give you a little more room at that end?"

"The grate is iron. Insanely heavy. That's as far as I could move it."

"But if you had help—"

"Hey, Mags!"

Brad twisted his head around and saw a couple of Maggie's fire department buddies clambering from a pickup truck. "Maggie, there was no need to call—"

"Relax. They're off duty."

"Those kids' books all talk about rescuing kittens from trees, not sewers," Ted joked, craning his neck for a good look. He squatted next to Brad. "How do you want to do this, Cat Guy?"

Brad bristled, but this wasn't the time or place for measuring tapes. He sucked in a deep breath, then slowly exhaled before answering. "I'd like to put something behind the cat, so he can't scoot into the pipe."

"Okay...Maggie gets on this end with a towel. We slide this thing farther out of the way—"

"Quietly, please, so he doesn't spook." He set down the can so his hand would be free to hopefully grab the cat if he bolted his way.

Ted and his buddies got into position to shift the grate. Maggie stationed herself at the end of the drain with a towel in case the cat went that way.

"One...two...three!"

The grate shifted suddenly, Maggie dove forward to block off the pipe, and the cat shot toward Brad, who caught him by the scruff of the neck, like a mama cat would. He rolled onto his back, cradling the bristling cat against his chest.

"Maggie, hold the cage. He's not gonna be happy about this."

Together, they wrestled the cat into the cage and shut the lid securely. Brad hauled himself out of the drain and sat on the pavement, panting. He wiped his forehead on his arm, wincing at the combination of abraded skin and sweat.

"Why don't you two take Miss Kitty inside, and we'll clean this up?" Ted suggested.

"Oh, you don't—" Brad began.

"Nah, it's cool," one of the guys said, grinning. "I get to tell my kid I helped the Cat Guy with one of his rescues."

****

Maggie didn't say a word the whole way down to the basement isolation room. She whispered soothing nonsense to the cat while Brad gathered supplies. She held her peace until he returned and carefully extracted the cat from the cage to assess its condition.

"So, tell me, did you find your first-aid certification in the bottom of a cereal box?"

"What?" He didn't look away from the cat. He hunkered on the counter, swathed in a towel from the carrier.

"The first thing you learn in any form of emergency training is to assess the situation. If you're not properly trained or equipped, you call in someone who is." She tore open an alcohol wipe and dabbed at the biggest scrape on his arm.

He winced, still focused on the cat. "I wasn't going to call the fire department to get a cat out of a storm drain."

"So you risked injury so you wouldn't have to deal with teasing from the guys?" She pressed a gauze pad to the oozing scrape.

"No." He finally turned to look at her. The cat remained frozen in place, eyes darting from side to side. He seemed wary but not terrified at his current situation. "Their job is to take care of people. I didn't want to draw off resources for something I could do myself."

"Except you obviously couldn't. And you didn't have to call 911. You could have come to me, and I would have gotten a couple of off-duty friends. Which is what I did anyway, but if you'd come to me first, maybe you wouldn't have gotten so banged up."

"I'm fine." He kept one hand on the cat and tried to make notes on a steno pad with the other.

"Give me that." She grabbed the pad and pen and glanced at him; one eyebrow raised.

"No fleas. No sign of other external parasites."

She noted that on the pad.

He checked the cat's ears. "No ear tip or tattoo."

"I thought we were friends."

His hands stilled on the cat, and he darted a glance at her. "We are."

"And you didn't stop to think how I'd feel when I looked out the window and saw you sprawled on the ground?"

"I…no…I guess I didn't. I'm sorry."

"Hold still." She grabbed his chin so she could dab at a small cut over his eye. "You need to wash your face before you scare anyone else. This is really tiny, though. It shouldn't leave a scar."

"Good. My arms are bad enough from the cats."

She scanned him with a professional eye. "Take off your shirt."

"Huh?"

"So I can clean and bandage the rest of those scrapes." Her cheeks flamed.

Brad gave himself a once-over. "No point, really. Bandages will come off in the shower. And I need one."

"Fine. Go ahead. I'll wait."

And now it was his turn to blush. "Er…I can take care of these myself."

"You can't see all of them."

"Hollyn can—"

"She's not home. Now leave the kitty to settle down and go take a shower."

"But I need to—"

"To let the poor cat have peace and quiet to calm down. I can do that."

When he hesitated, she grabbed a handful of his grubby T-shirt and pulled him close for a fierce kiss. Then she shoved him away lightly. She laid a gentle hand on the towel covering the cat.

"Cat. Shower. Now."

"Yes, ma'am."

"I'll settle him in the isolation room for now."

Brad paused at the door. "He'll need—"

"A litter box, food, and water. I'll figure it out. Your sister labels everything really well. Now go."

****

Maggie sat curled in the corner of the couch, absorbed in a graphic novel with Mocha snuggled beside her. Once again, she had the oddest feeling she was more comfortable here than in her own apartment. Definitely more comfortable than she'd ever been in Jack's fancy condo. A home should be—well, homelike. Not a showplace. She liked curling up on the couch without worrying about marking the upholstery. She liked bookcases crammed with books worn from being read and reread, not titles chosen because they'd look sophisticated.

She was growing accustomed to the rhythm of the house. A kitty's paws skittered across the kitchen tiles, and Mocha's contented purrs rumbled against her hip. The shower shut off a little while ago. What the heck was taking him so long?

She heard the faintest creak from the staircase and

glanced across the room. There he was—barefoot, shirt in hand, and his hair damp from the shower. *Wow*. He wasn't heavily muscled, but she'd never found that type attractive anyway. He looked like someone who knew how to give excellent hugs and cuddles. And if a bit of cuddling happened to lead to other…no. Nope.

Down girl. You're supposed to be mad at him.

Brad looked slightly confused—but not at all unhappy—to see her ensconced in his living room. She took pity on him.

"Hollyn's downstairs looking after Miss Kitty, Elsie's outside feeding the guys, and Chief Parker walked Mr. Carson to his house so he could write him a bunch of citations."

He blinked. "I didn't think I was in the shower that long. And how did Chief Parker and Mr. Carson become involved in this?"

"Well, you were pretty grubby." Maggie eyed him. "Apparently Mr. Carson called the police to complain about Ted's truck."

"Which is parked legally on a public street."

She nodded. "Yeah. Meanwhile, the guy who runs the ice cream truck called in a complaint about Cuthbert harassing his customers. One kid's father is threatening a lawsuit. I think Chief Parker was inventing new charges on the spot. He especially wanted to write a ticket for Cuthbert lifting his leg on the police cruiser."

"Wow."

"Now come over here so I can take a look at you…I mean, at the damage you managed to inflict on yourself."

****

Maggie flushed an adorable shade of pink at her faux pas. Brad chose not to comment. *I like seeing her here. She looks like she belongs.* He could have protested that none of the injuries were severe enough to need attention, but if the beautiful lady paramedic wanted to…uh-uh. Nope. *So* inappropriate. Maggie was a thorough professional who most definitely would not appreciate the direction his mind was wandering. Besides, she might spot something he couldn't see or reach.

He padded down the rest of the stairs and crossed the room to sit beside her on the couch. She already had supplies laid out on a towel on the coffee table.

She gently prodded a couple of angry scratches on his chest. "When did she manage to tag you?"

"When I lifted him out of the drain. Can't say as I blame him. I was so afraid he'd escape I probably grabbed him too tightly."

"Her. Hollyn says the cat is a girl. And also, kitten season may not be over yet." She swiped at the scratches with an antiseptic wipe.

He winced. "Well, it's not like I was paying attention to that end of the cat at the time."

"Hollyn thinks maybe Miss Kitty isn't feral. She's scrawny, like maybe she doesn't know how to hunt. She knows food comes from a can and goes in a dish. And she knows how to use the litter box." She appraised his injuries with a cool, professional eye. "Most of the bleeding has stopped, and none of them are deep. Do you want to bandage any of these?"

He twisted his arms, surveying the damage. "Nah. The tape'll hurt worse than the actual scrapes. What about you? Did you emerge from your first cat rescue unscathed?"

"I'm fine. I just wish you'd come over and asked me

for help. I do this sort of thing for a living, you know."

"I didn't want to bother you. You didn't sign up for the day-to-day mess this job entails. And I know you work crazy shifts and need your rest."

"And I'm perfectly capable of telling you if I need to spend the day sleeping." She laid her hand on Brad's shoulder and pressed a soft kiss to the corner of his mouth. "Quit showing off. You know how you keep telling me I don't need to prove how tough I am? Well, neither do you. I like you just fine the way you are."

Brad froze, his dark eyes fixed on hers while her thumb traced small shapes on his shoulder. His throat worked for a moment before he spoke. "I like you, too. But I…I don't want to be rebound guy. That never works out well for me. I know that sounds selfish, but I'm tired of being someone's second choice."

Maggie leaned in closer. "You're not. I'm here because I want to be—because I want to be with you." She snaked her other arm up to cup his cheek. "I didn't come here looking to fall for anyone, and yet, here you are, with your books and your kittens and…" She pulled his head down and pressed her lips to his. "I'm so glad I found you."

He edged closer on the sofa and slid an arm around her, pulling her firmly into his space. "Me, too."

She smiled at him, and he leaned in and kissed that smile right off her lips. Her lips parted sweetly under his—she must have found Hollyn's chocolate stash. His free hand tangled in her curls, the silken strands slipping through his fingers. Maggie leaned on a toy that squeaked, and she laughed against his mouth. Her arms wound around his neck, and she shifted almost onto his lap. It had been a while since he did this sort of thing, and his nerves sang with exquisite sensations. She was so warm and soft against his skin…well, except for the buttons on her flannel shirt which stung against his cuts and scrapes. His hand drifted to her collar—

The front door thumped open. "Hey, Brad—did you bring in all the mail? I can't find— Oh, fudgebuckets!" The door slammed shut.

They broke apart.

"Was that—?" Maggie ran a hand through her hair.

"My beloved sister. Yup." He reached for the shirt he'd dropped on the coffee table.

"No—she went back out. Was that Nixie?"

He dragged the shirt over his head and sucked in a deep breath, trying to calm his heart rate…among other bodily functions.

Maggie rose to her feet, looking as breathless as he felt. "We should go help."

"She doesn't usually go too far, but yeah. You're right." *Of course she's right. But…damn…*

She reached up and wiped a smudge of lip gloss from the corner of his mouth with her thumb. "We can continue this conversation another time." Her green eyes sparkled with merriment.

He cleared his throat twice before he trusted his voice. "I'd like that."

Chapter Thirteen

Maggie checked her appearance in the mirror. She'd tamed her curls into a French braid and applied a minimal amount of makeup. She tugged her uniform jacket straight. Calm, cool, and professional—exactly the impression she wanted to make for her first time recording a PSA for the local cable station.

Ted shoved her aside good-naturedly. "Does this uniform make me look fat?"

"No, but all the candy you're shoveling in might." She eyed the picked-over craft services table. "Leave some for the rest of us. And maybe comb your hair?"

He swiped a hand over his head, which left his hair even more ruffled. "Is your boyfriend here yet? He and his sister have a segment, don't they?"

"Yes, they do, and he's not my boyfriend. Do you even own a comb?"

"Maybe." Another ineffectual swipe. "Why the hell not? You should ask him to the thing."

"You don't think less than a week is awfully short notice?"

"Why? He doesn't have to rent a tux or anything. A suit'll do fine."

"He might have plans."

"You won't know unless you ask." He started counting off reasons on his fingers. "He's a decent guy. He's sure as hell never gonna tell you his job is more important than yours—unlike what's-his-face. And you spend all your free time at his house anyway. Except for when you go to the diner. Boyfriend."

"He's—we're—he's not." Heat crept up her neck at the sudden visceral mental image of a shirtless Brad—and the warm solidity of his body against hers, even through her fall layers. And how warm and soft his lips were. She shook her head sharply. "And how do you even know we've been to the diner?"

Ted rolled his eyes. "Please. For one thing, there's not a whole helluva lot of places to go around here. And for another, Millie brought over a buncha coffees to the station, and she mighta mentioned seeing you. And then there's Gus the window washer, and the high school kids have been hanging posters and flyers for the Halloween events—"

And then the green room door opened, and a PA ushered Brad and Hollyn in. Maggie's flush escalated to a total body red-alert. She ran a finger inside her uniform collar.

The siblings were better dressed and groomed than usual. Hollyn wore light makeup and carried a crisp white lab coat over one arm. Brad wore a bulky, blue wool cable knit-sweater over an autumn-toned plaid shirt. The colors brought out his warm brown eyes.

Which I really should stop staring at.

Brad's face lit up as soon as he saw her. "Do you guys have a segment, too?"

"Yeah. You folks sure take your holidays seriously here."

"Well, Carson Mills is a nice place for families. The streets are safe for trick or treating, and there's a seriously scary haunted house in the high school gym to keep the older kids out of mischief."

"Oh, right—they advertised it at the parade, didn't they?"

"They did." He looked like he wanted to say more, but his gaze darted between Ted and his sister, then he rather obviously changed the subject. "What's your segment about?"

"Safe Halloween decorating. It's a variation on one of the Christmas PSAs. Secure your extension cords, don't overload the circuits, maintain clear paths—you get the idea. What about you?"

"The usual." He ticked off items on his fingers. "Chocolate is toxic to pets. Prepare a saferoom so your pet can't escape or be frightened by costumes and strange noises. Be sure to keep your black cats and dogs safely at home."

She shuddered. "Is that really an issue here?"

Hollyn shrugged into her lab coat. "We don't get a lot of the nasty stuff in Carson Mills, thank God, but it's always a good thing to keep in mind. A more likely scenario around here is a dark-furred animal spooking, darting into the road, and running in front of a car."

"How's the drain kitty?" Ted asked.

"Pregnant," Hollyn replied. "Very, very pregnant."

Ted looked confused. "But Cat Guy here kept calling him a boy."

Brad rolled his eyes. "I'm never gonna live that down, am I?"

Hollyn chortled gleefully. "Nope."

Ted glanced from one sibling to the other, obviously perplexed. "Don't pregnant cats get—

you know—" He made a rounded sort of gesture.

"Okay, in my brother's defense, he was more

concerned with Miss Kitty not hot-footing it into the sewer system. He probably would have spotted all the super obvious signs himself if he'd done the intake, but he didn't. And she's not very round because she hasn't been eating enough. We're trying to put weight on her before she goes into labor."

Ted grinned. "Well, if anyone can help her, it's you guys."

A rosy blush spread over Hollyn's cheeks and the room grew weirdly silent.

"Who's on now?" Brad asked to break the unnatural hush.

"Chief Parker," Ted replied, sliding right back into his casual familiarity. "He already did the curfew and safe trick or treating. I think he's recording the traffic safety one now. Your favorite neighbor did his opinion piece earlier."

"What was it this time? Banning trick or treat again? Or has he escalated to canceling Christmas?"

"Who cares?" Ted waved a hand carelessly. "The fastest way for the channel to be changed is for his ugly mug to appear on screen."

Brad sidled a bit closer to Maggie. "Thanks for helping us catch Nixie."

"I can't believe the little stinker was hiding under the rocking chair while we were crawling all over the yard."

"Good thing you thought of opening the can of stinky tuna, or we might still be out there."

A small half smile twitched at her lips. "There are worse things."

He glanced down at his shoes, then back at her. "Um…you look really nice."

"Thanks. We don't usually manage to stay this tidy on an actual shift. No T-shirt today?" She studied Brad appreciatively. His brown hair had faint coppery highlights. *I never noticed that before.*

He shrugged. "Hollyn says I can't go on TV unless I dress like a competent professional."

"If I've gotta wear this stupid thing," Hollyn grumbled, tugging the lab coat into place, "you can survive in grown-up clothes for a few hours."

From across the room, Ted mouthed "boyfriend."

Maggie ignored him. She glanced at Brad through her lashes. Maybe she would invite him—

The door opened again, and a PA with a clipboard and headset appeared. "Can we have the representatives from the fire department, please?"

Brad smiled and squeezed her arm gently. "Knock 'em dead."

****

The following morning, Brad flung open the front door, expecting a delivery. It was—just not the one he was expecting. "Maggie—hi, come on in. Didn't I give you a key?"

"Well, yeah, but I feel weird just walking in."

"Don't," he told her with a warm grin. "Like I said, you're part of the team now."

He and Se blinked at the commotion, then jumped down and ran over when they recognized Maggie. They pounced at the crinkly plastic shopping bags she carried, snagging one right out of her hand.

"What's this?" Brad stooped to recover the contents.

"Well, I was at the mall, buying a few things for my apartment and I saw towels on final clearance. I warn you, they're butt ugly, but they were super cheap, and I know how many you go through around here. I hope that's okay?"

"God, yes. Don't get me wrong, I'm grateful for every donation we receive, but people do tend to drift toward the cute toys and accessories."

"Good. I'm glad they'll be useful."

"Did you save your receipt? I'll give you a donation slip."

"You don't need to—"

"Actually, I do. The Clowder is a registered not-for-profit." He jerked his head toward the permits on the wall.

She handed over the receipt reluctantly. "Anything else I should keep an eye out for?"

He sat at the computer and opened a form. "Really good deals on paper towels, garbage bags, and laundry detergent."

"You should have a wish list." Maggie smiled at a postcard stuck in the corner of the doorframe—kittens dressed in football jerseys.

"We do…a general one on The Clowder's website and registries with a couple of online places. Like I said, folks are very generous. It's just…when people watch on their computers, it's easy to think this is all fun and cuddles and cute toys. But unfortunately, there's also poop and barf, and sometimes things don't have a happy ending." He shut his mouth abruptly. "Sorry."

"Don't be." She studied him thoughtfully for a moment. "Are you worried about Miss Kitty?"

He nodded. "She's small and thin, and Hollyn thinks she's very young. We're working on getting her stronger, but sometimes a young cat doesn't have the instincts to deliver or care for her kittens. Or they could be underweight or underdeveloped or—"

She laid her hand on his arm and squeezed gently. "Hey. Are you and Hollyn doing everything in your power to help her?"

He nodded decisively. "We are."

"I believe in you." She leaned down and dropped a light kiss on his forehead.

Brad's mouth curled into a crooked smile. "Thanks. That means a lot." He finished typing and hit print. "That'll print at my desk."

"Where should I put these?" Maggie reclaimed the bags from He and Se.

"Oh, you can just leave them—" Brad began.

"No. I'm part of the team, remember? Where do they belong?"

"Upstairs linen closet."

"Cool. I can visit Cosmos and Nebula."

"They're always happy to see you. Er…I mean, all of us are…"

Maggie smirked ever so slightly. "So…just out of curiosity, do you own a suit?"

"Uh…yeah? I mean, I can't recall the last time I actually wore one…"

"It takes a lot to persuade him to dress like an actual adult," Hollyn interjected, barging into the hall. "Brad, are there any clean towels anywhere in this house?"

"Funny you should ask." He lobbed a bag at her.

"Oh my God…my eyes…" she whined, rifling through the puce green and mustard yellow contents.

"That's probably why they were on clearance," Maggie informed her. "Besides, I've seen the state of most of your towels. These at least don't have holes."

"True," Hollyn agreed.

"Was there something you needed the towels for?" Brad hinted. "Something happening in another room, maybe?"

Hollyn smirked gleefully. "I'm going to be clattering up and down the stairs—very noisily—getting stuff for Miss Kitty's room. I might also run the washer and dryer—again, very noisily. So I couldn't possibly hear anything else going on in the house."

Brad fixed her with a long-suffering stare. "You know, when Mom said I was going to have a baby sister, I asked if I could have a puppy instead."

Hollyn stuck her tongue out at him and retreated upstairs with her bag of towels. Brad shook his head.

"I'm sorry, Maggie…what were you were saying before we were treated to the Hollyn MacKenzie Not-So-Funny Show?"

She stifled the last of her giggles. "Well…I know this is awfully short notice, but there's an event coming up. Saturday night, actually. The Firefighter's Memorial Ball is a fundraiser for the families of firefighters lost in the line of duty. Um…I usually go alone, but I'm receiving a citation this year, and I thought it might be nice…I mean, if you're not busy…"

"Are you asking me on a date? Like a date-date?"

"Yeah. I guess I am."

"A ball, huh? How's the whole fire department get the same night off?"

"We swap with other departments. So, are you interested?"

Brad waggled his eyebrows. "Let's see…a whole uninterrupted evening of not cleaning hairballs or litter boxes? You in a pretty dress? Hell yeah, I'm interested."

"All right then…it's a date."

"I promise I'll wear shoes and everything."

Chapter Fourteen

Maggie rifled through the few remaining dresses in her closet. She selected a soft lilac cocktail dress with its original tags still attached. "What do you think?"

"I love the color." Hollyn slouched more comfortably into the room's only chair. "I can't remember the last time I got dolled up like that."

"Prom?"

"Nah. There was a science fair that weekend which did not require stuffing my feet into high heels or the rest of me into shapewear."

Maggie eyed her critically. "You don't need shapewear. There are plenty of styles that work fine without. You just have to find the right cut to suit your body."

Hollyn snorted. "Too much hassle. And where do I go that requires a fancy dress?"

Maggie shrugged. "You never know."

"How do you know so much about this, anyway?"

Maggie froze in the act of hanging the dress in the closet. "Jack—my ex—took me to all sorts of high-end business dinners and parties. He said it made him look bad if I wore the same outfit too often." She snuck a look at Hollyn, comfy in her ubiquitous rumpled scrubs and sneakers.

She looked as though she was struggling to formulate a polite comment. "Was it fun, at least?"

"Maybe at first. I mean, who doesn't want to do the whole fairy tale princess thing?"

"Me, that's who."

"Actually, it got old pretty fast. I mean, dressing up and going out is nice every once in a while, but not all the time, and not with no regard for my work schedule." She paid a great deal of attention to making sure the dress hung straight in the closet, with space so it wouldn't wrinkle. "Any time I had a work event, Jack had a schedule conflict. No one really notices if you're alone at a barbeque, but they do notice if you walk into a ball by yourself."

Hollyn winced. "Ouch."

"So then I was stuck at the misfit's table with Ted."

"Your partner? He seems like a nice enough guy."

"Yeah, but I spend forty hours a week with him. That's like going on a date with your brother."

"Point taken."

Maggie sucked in a deep breath and plastered a smile on her face. "I like doing things where I can wear whatever I want without worrying about getting messy."

"Well, you'll fit right in with us. And no offense, but your ex sounds like a prize jerk."

"So I've been told. When I moved out, I donated most of the fancy outfits to an organization that provides prom dresses to underprivileged kids."

Hollyn snickered.

Maggie shook off the past. "So—the lilac?"

"Definitely."

****

"Brad, did you take your suit to the dry cleaners?" Hollyn demanded through the closed door of Miss Kitty's nursery.

"Um…yeah." He petted the mama cat gently with a long-handled brush. She was much less skittish, thanks to Elsie's unrelenting regimen of love and cuddles. "How much did you say she weighs?"

"About eight pounds."

"That's…not good."

"No, it isn't. And did you go to the store?"

"For what?"

"A new white shirt. I can't even remember the last time you wore one. And you need to polish your shoes."

"Anything else?"

"Get a haircut," Elsie interjected, looking around the door to the linen closet.

"You too?" Brad whined. *Seriously? What's wrong with my hair? It's still short enough to stay out of my eyes when I shove it back.*

"This is very important to Maggie," Elsie scolded.

"I know."

"I don't think you do," Hollyn retorted. "Her ex was a jerk who never went to any of her work events—even though he threw a hissy fit if she missed one of his. Most of the fire department occasions are community service or picnic sort of things. This is the only fancy one, and Maggie never had someone go with her before. This event is important to her, and I like having her as a friend, so I'd appreciate if you didn't screw this up." Hollyn paused. "Brad, are you listening to me?" She stamped her foot. "Do you care about Maggie?"

"Of course I do."

Her expression gentled. "It's not enough for her to like the things you like. You have to put effort into this relationship, too."

"I don't know how to do this, all right? I never

have."

"Well, in this case, it's easy," Elsie informed him, moving beside Hollyn. "You wear your suit and take Maggie to this party and smile and be nice to her colleagues. You're a published author. Surely you can manage a few hours of polite conversation with pleasant people. You've already met a lot of them."

Well. Put that way, a couple hours wasn't such a big deal. And smiling and chatting with Maggie's colleagues would make her happy. And he really did love her smiles...

The door opened, and Elsie padded into the room.

"I'll look after Miss Kitty for a while. You go into town and do what you need to do to show Maggie how special she is. Remember, she chose you. Now you must return the favor."

Chapter Fifteen

Maggie rang the bell for the third time. When no one came to open the door, she fished out her key and let herself in.

"Brad?" She shut the door and wandered inside. He wasn't at his table in the living room, although Mocha was curled in his chair. He hopped down and trotted over to the food bowl where he meowed expectantly.

"Sorry, buddy, but I'm not coming near you in this dress. Brad?" she called again.

The light in the upstairs landing was on, dimly illuminating the steps. She shrugged out of her coat and laid it over the back of the couch. "Don't even think about it," she warned Nixie before heading upstairs.

A wash of brighter light spilled from the doorway of Miss Kitty's nursery. Maggie checked the note on the door—security cam only. She tapped lightly on the glass, then slipped off her heels and entered carefully.

Brad's head and shoulders disappeared inside a cabinet that had been converted into a cozy nest. He wore ragged jeans and a thoroughly disreputable T-shirt. A bloody towel and a plastic bowl of something she didn't care to contemplate too closely sat on the floor next to him.

"Brad? You're not dressed."

"I'm dressed…just not the way you want me to be." The walls of the cabinet muffled his voice.

The occupant of the nest loosed an unearthly yowl.

"I know, baby," he muttered. "I know it hurts. You're doing so well."

"Brad, do you have any idea what time it is?"

"Um…actually…no."

"Brad!"

****

He carefully extricated his head from the nest and craned his neck to see her. She shaded her eyes, and he snapped off his headlamp. Sweat dampened his hair—so much for the fresh haircut.

Maggie wore a lilac-colored dress that clung softly to her figure. Her curls were carefully arranged, and there were complicated makeup things happening he didn't know the proper terms for.

"Wow. You look amazing."

"You don't."

"Look, I'm sorry, but this is totally beyond my control." He pulled off the headlamp and wiped his forehead on his sleeve.

"You know how important this is to me."

"I do. You're receiving a commendation you totally deserve."

"And you were supposed to be there for me."

Brad sighed heavily, turning his head slightly to watch Miss Kitty out of the corner of his eye. "I'm sorry. I really am, but it's not like I planned this. She's been laboring for hours, and she's tired. There are still a couple more kittens in there. I can't just walk away."

"Isn't there anyone else?"

He shook his head. "Hollyn had to cover a shift at the emergency clinic tonight, and I'd never leave Elsie alone with something like this. I'm sorry." He squirmed, trying to stretch out a crick in his spine. "You should go on without me. You don't want to be late to your own party."

"It's not my party—it's the Firefighter's—"

"—Memorial Ball. I know." This was a huge deal for her. He knew that. But the combination of the fancy dress and careful hair and makeup made her seem like a stranger—someone distant and unattainable.

"How long do you think you'll be? Maybe we could arrive fashionably late."

"I don't know. This isn't an exact science. And I need to monitor the babies. She's too tired to deal with the placentas herself. I need to make sure they're able to nurse."

Miss Kitty wailed again. Brad returned his full attention to the cat and the tiny squeaking babies she'd already delivered.

"I'm sorry, but this is what I do. These are living things. My job doesn't stop because it's a holiday or I have plans, or I'd rather be out with my girlfriend. I know your job is important, and tonight is special, but what I do matters, too."

He didn't look up, but he heard the sharp final snap of the door shutting behind her.

****

Brad slept fitfully, propped against the wall next to Miss Kitty's nest. The sound of movement somewhere in the house filtered vaguely into his awareness, and then someone shook his shoulder.

"Hey," Hollyn said by way of greeting.

He mumbled an unintelligible response. Hollyn shoved a little harder, and he awoke with a snort.

"Have you been in here all night?"

"I dunno…what time is it?"

"A little after five."

A strong scent of peppermint pervaded the room, and he tracked it to the steaming mug in Hollyn's hands. "Since when do you drink tea?"

"Since I need to clear the smell of ear pus out of my nose. 'Cuz, you know—two a.m. Sunday morning is the perfect time to decide you can't wait another moment to seek care for an ear infection that's obviously been raging for weeks. I don't know how they stood the stink for so long." She eyed him critically. "Didn't you shave?"

"Um…no."

"You had a date last night, a fancy one, and you didn't shave?"

"No. In my defense, I didn't actually go on the date, so no one noticed I hadn't shaved."

"Brad, what the hell is wrong with you? Last night was a big deal for Maggie."

"If you could not yell at me, it would be really great." He groaned and scrubbed at his face. "Maggie yelled at me plenty last night. Besides, as you can see, this wasn't exactly my choice."

She made an affirmative sort of sound and hunkered down to look inside the nest, where three tiny kittens nestled against their mama's side. "Is this all of them?"

"I hope so. It's been about five hours."

"Were they all live births?"

Brad shook his head and gestured to a tiny shape wrapped in a clean white face cloth on the counter.

"I'm sorry," Hollyn murmured. "You could have called me."

"You were working."

129

"You could have brought them to me."

"She was having trouble. If I transported her, she would have been on her own for the entire ride. I might have lost all of them."

Hollyn sighed heavily. "How mad is Maggie?"

"Somewhere north of furious."

"Ouch."

"Pretty much. See, this is why I don't date. When I bring in an animal, it's a commitment. I can't just take off because something more interesting is happening."

"You don't need to explain to me." She took a gulp of her tea and made a face. "Why don't you clean up and sleep in an actual bed for a while?"

Brad groaned as he hauled himself to his feet. "I need to take care of this mess first." He waved his hand vaguely at the used towels and plastic bowl of placentas.

"I'll do it."

"You've been awake all night."

"Yeah, but my night wasn't as exciting as yours. Go on. I'll leave a note for Elsie to wake you first when she gets here."

Brad rubbed his eye with the heel of his hand. "All right."

"Have they all nursed?"

"I think so. I started a weight chart. Sorry...it's kinda messy."

Hollyn waved him off. "If I was fazed by that sort of mess, I'd have picked a different career. Mama's okay?"

"Tired, but she ate...looks like the whole dish I gave her."

"I'll give her a refill. Think this is the last litter for the season?"

"I hope so."

"We did good work this year."

"We did, but we could all use a break."

She grabbed a can of food and popped the lid open. "After you've rested, you really ought to talk to Maggie."

"About what? This is my life. She's upset about last night, and she's certainly entitled, but…"

"I know, but I like her, and I know you do too…I just…I think she'd understand if you talked to her. Don't be so quick to give up, okay?"

"Okay," Brad agreed wearily.

"Go on," Hollyn said, giving him a gentle shove. "Go get some sleep and maybe even—"

"Shower?"

She wrinkled her nose. "It certainly wouldn't hurt."

****

Brad dimly became aware of someone tapping on the door to the attic stairs.

"Brad? Are you alive up there?" Elsie called.

He groaned. "Um…I guess so. Be down in a few."

"All right. I brought cinnamon buns, and I'll start coffee."

"Thanks, Elsie," he mumbled.

His rumpled bed offered the alluring promise of sleep, but no…he needed to check on the babies. Not to mention deal with the aftermath of last night's failed date. He dragged himself from bed and rifled through the pile of unfolded laundry, looking for a clean pair of jeans. Rain spattered against the window and the October morning was chill and damp enough that he added a flannel shirt and a pair of thick woolen socks.

His suit, still in the dry cleaner's plastic, hung on the

outside of the closet door, an uncomfortable reminder of the fun conversation he had to look forward to. *Later. Much later, after at least one pot of coffee. And where the hell is my phone? The heck with it…coffee first.*

He stumbled down the stairs to the second floor. Hollyn had stuck sticky notes with updates on the door to Miss Kitty's room. He scanned them quickly. Mama had eaten, and all the kittens had latched. He checked for himself anyway.

Mama snoozed with her brood curled against her. Brad blinked and rubbed his eyes, then counted again. Yup, there were four kittens now. Miss Kitty appeared to have delivered the last on her own and dealt with the placenta. He refilled her bowl and added notes to her file.

He followed the aroma of fresh coffee to the kitchen. Elsie bustled around, looking after He and Se and trying to keep Nixie out of the people food. She eyed him sympathetically.

"I knew there was something wrong when I walked in, and there was no coffee."

"Yeah…that's never a good sign around here."

Elsie slid a mug in his direction. "How bad was the birth?"

Brad took a long, fortifying sip before answering. "It wasn't the worst we've had, but…I lost one."

"I'm so sorry. When did she go into labor?"

"Oh, you know…about half an hour after Hollyn was called to cover a shift at the emergency hospital."

"Of course." Elsie sighed and set Nixie on the floor. "I gather from the look of you that you didn't have a chance to go to Maggie's party."

"I did not." He gulped more coffee, waiting for the bitter jolt of caffeine to overcome the lack of sleep.

"How upset is she?"

"Very."

"You need to talk to her."

"So I've been told."

Hollyn shambled into the kitchen, drawn by the siren song of fresh coffee. "Are my eyes going funny?"

"Probably, but yes, you actually did see one more kitten than you remembered." Brad passed her a mug of coffee and refilled his own.

"Have you talked to Maggie yet?"

Brad gestured vaguely with his mug.

"I don't think your brother is awake yet, dear," Elsie said.

He wandered over to the window, still sipping his coffee. He glanced aimlessly around the yard, then caught sight of a small dark shape. He set his mug on the windowsill and squinted. Then he snatched a pair of gloves from the nearest box.

"Hollyn, grab a couple of towels, would you?" he said as he jammed his feet into a pair of old sneakers lying on the floor by the door.

"Huh?" Then she stepped beside him to see what he was looking at. "Oooohhhh crud."

****

The dank gray day matched Maggie's mood all too well. She threw herself into her work so she wouldn't have to think about the night before. She announced her intention to reorganize the supply room and proceeded to sort and catalog supplies with ruthless efficiency. Most of the guys had noticed her lack of escort at the party and gave her a wide berth. With one notable exception, of course. She looked up and saw Ted lounging in the doorway, donut in hand.

"I don't think I've ever seen this room look so good," he remarked, munching away.

"Don't start."

"Look, Mags…I know you're upset. But did you at least talk to him? Did he have a reason? He doesn't seem like the kind of guy who'd blow off something he knew was so important to you."

An uncomfortable blush crept up her neck.

"Maggie?" Ted prompted.

"Remember the cat we helped him get out of the storm drain?"

Ted nodded, unfazed by the seeming non sequitur.

"Well, she went into labor last night."

"Don't animals do that by instinct? Don't look at me like that—I read."

"Usually, yes, but this was…complicated."

Ted eyed her shrewdly. "So let me see if I've got this straight—your boyfriend couldn't go to the ball with you last night because he was handling a life-or-death emergency at his own job?"

By this point, her cheeks were absolutely blazing.

Ted crossed his arms and stared at her. "Maggie, you have to call him. This wasn't another case of Jack being a jackass. The guy had a reason—a good one. Just like you had good reasons whenever you needed to bail. It works both ways, you know."

"I do know," she admitted miserably. "It's just…after all the times Jack blew off my events, I finally thought…"

"Hey—you're absolutely entitled to be disappointed about last night. But you gotta keep in mind he didn't stand you up on purpose. Everybody loves to see the adorable pictures of kittens Brad posts, but after you've been following him a while, you realize as adorable as the cute stuff is, the sad stuff…well, it can be just as hard as what we deal with. So look, I'm just saying—it sounds like he had a rough night, too, and you really need to talk to him."

Maggie shuffled boxes of gauze around on the shelf so she wouldn't have to meet Ted's eyes. "So basically…I turned into Jack?"

"Oh, hell no. It takes a lifetime of dedicated work to achieve that level of jerkdom. You got upset. It happens. Just don't let things fester."

Maggie nodded.

"Look, I'll even close the door so you can make a phone call in privacy." Ted winked at her, then shut the door with a soft click.

Maggie sucked in a deep breath, then pulled out her phone and dialed Brad.

****

Brad's eyes stung as he looked at the damp, bedraggled cat on the basement counter. He knew he couldn't save all of them, but every loss still stung, especially when this one died right in his backyard before he had the chance to help her.

Hollyn frowned as she examined the cat. "She's given birth recently. She has milk, and there's a bit of a mess around her tail. So much for kitten season being over."

"Is there any way to tell how long ago she delivered?"

"Sure. Let me consult my crystal ball."

"Hollyn…"

His sister leveled a flat stare in his general direction. "Recently. That's the best I can tell."

"So there could be babies out there."

She sighed heavily. "Brad, you don't know where to start looking for a nest. It's wet and windy outside—how long do you think fragile newborns can last without a mama cat to keep them warm?"

"Not long at all. That's why I have to move."

He grabbed a carrier with a shoulder strap and tossed in a couple of towels. He clicked on a flashlight to check the batteries, then tucked it into his pocket.

"Can you look after her?" he asked.

"Of course, but—"

"I'll be back as soon as I find them."

"Will you at least put on a decent jacket and boots?"

"I'm not taking the time to go hunting for boots." He hauled himself up the steps.

"Brad!"

Chapter Sixteen

Maggie shivered in the wind as she hesitated at the door to Brad's house. Water dripped down the sides of the lovingly carved jack-o-lanterns on the steps. A plastic skull blew loose from someone's yard display and skittered down the center of the road. For the first time, she doubted her welcome. She steeled herself and pushed the door open, keeping a firm grip so it wouldn't fly out of her hand.

"Brad? Is that you?" Elsie called from upstairs.

"It's Maggie."

Elsie came down the stairs a moment later. She walked right to Maggie and enfolded her in a comforting embrace. Maggie allowed herself a moment to enjoy the hug.

"Um…I've been trying to call Brad all day. He's not answering his phone."

Elsie chuckled softly. "He stumbled down here half asleep late this morning. Heaven only knows where he left his phone."

"What's going on? Where is he?"

"He's in the woods looking for the babies." Elsie kept a comforting arm around her shoulders.

"But…the babies were upstairs in the nest?"

"Miss Kitty's are—" Elsie corrected herself. "—but Brad and Hollyn found a mama cat in the yard this morning. She looked like she'd given birth recently.

137

Hollyn had to run to her office for an appointment. Brad's still out searching for the nest."

"Couldn't he follow the mama cat?"

"No, dear." Elsie's kind eyes shimmered with unshed tears.

"What…oh. He must be so…and I said things last night…"

Elsie gripped her arms firmly. "You both have a right to be upset about last night, and you need to have a serious conversation about that, but right now—"

"Right now, I need to find Brad."

Elsie smiled tightly and nodded. "Are you warm enough?"

Maggie nodded, indicating her uniform. "I came straight from work. Any idea which way he went?"

Elsie led her to the kitchen window and pointed. "Brad set that bucket where they found the mama cat."

"Thanks." Maggie slipped a clean pair of exam gloves into her pocket. "I have my phone, and it's charged."

"Call me if you need help. I'll send Hollyn out when she gets back. Please be careful, dear."

"I will," Maggie promised.

****

The storm wasn't really heavy—yet—but everything was soaked and dripping—and cold. The chill sank deep into her bones. This kind of cold was deadly to tiny newborn kittens without a mother to keep them warm. Gusts of wind grew stronger and more frequent. Maggie's pants were soaked to the knees before she made it out of the yard.

The woods were worse. The pretty autumn leaves had fallen and faded, leaving everything a wash of brown and gray. She wished she'd thought to ask Elsie what Brad was wearing. *Rookie mistake. If you can't act like a professional, step back and call someone who can.*

She cupped her hands around her mouth. "Brad!" The raw wind snatched her words away.

She didn't see any sign of him, so she plodded further into the dripping underbrush. Water ran in her eyes, and she wiped the drops away irritably. *How far could he have gone? Focus. He's looking for kittens. They'll be on the ground. He's probably down on his hands and knees.*

She trudged farther through the trees, keeping her gaze low and looking for any sign of Brad. The woods seemed gray and forbidding today...like something that could gobble up tiny little lives...or even a human one. She shuddered and gauged the distance to the house. *How far could a dying cat have dragged herself? I should have checked a map to see how far these woods go.*

"Brad!" Again, silence. She glanced at her watch. *Five more minutes, then I'm calling for help.*

She called again, then froze. Was that a voice? She stilled, holding her breath, and tried to hear past the rush of the wind through the trees. The branches of a shrub to her left moved. *Bears? Please tell me there're no bears around here.* Nope. Not a bear—a bedraggled Brad straightened from where he'd been crouched under a shrub and waved. She hurried over to him, getting wetter—and colder—by the second. He wasn't really that far into the woods, but the dripping greenery had shrouded him until he stood.

"Are you okay? You look cold." *Well, isn't that the understatement of the century?* Rain plastered his hair to his head, his clothes were drenched, and there were dark smudges under his eyes.

"I'm all right. Look, Maggie…I just wanted—" He broke off, coughing.

"I shouldn't have said—"

"Maybe we should do this someplace drier."

"Have you found them?"

Brad shook his head, shivering.

"How long can they last out here?"

He wiped his nose with the cuff of his jacket and looked away. Maggie reached up and touched his face. His skin was clammy. Never a good sign.

"You need to get in out of this. Tell me where to look."

"They can't be far. The mother managed to drag herself into the backyard."

"She'd pick someplace sort of sheltered, right?" She scanned the surrounding area. "What about that?"

"That" was the partially rotted trunk of a fallen tree.

"Good eyes."

"I had a good teacher. But really—you're soaked and freezing. You should go back to the house."

Brad shook his head. "We're about to lose our window of opportunity. Babies can't thermoregulate. If we don't find them soon…"

She wrapped her warm hands around his frigid ones and breathed on them. "We will. If they're here, we'll find them."

They clambered over to the fallen log. Maggie extended her hand for the flashlight.

"Let me. I'm smaller."

"I'm already soaked," Brad protested. His teeth chattered.

"So am I. Hand it over."

She got down on her hands and knees in the mud and fallen leaves and used the flashlight to peer inside the log.

"Their eyes aren't open yet, so there won't be anything to reflect the light," he reminded her.

The interior of the log smelled vaguely mildewy. There were layers of leaves and—yuck—spider webs. And over there—was that deeper patch of darkness moving? Ever so slightly?

"They're back here."

"Be sure they're kittens and not skunks," Brad cautioned.

"I didn't think baby skunks sprayed."

"Not as good as their mama does, but is that really something you want to experiment with?"

"Point taken. Anyway, skunks don't come in tabby." She wrestled a pair of gloves onto her wet hands, then ducked down. "Get the carrier ready."

She stretched out her hand and grasped a kitten. The tiny creature flailed weakly, opening its mouth in a silent hiss. She passed the kitten to Brad, then reached for another. She added two more tabbies, a solid black kitten, and one that looked like a cow kitty.

Brad set them in a nest of towels in the carrier. "Is this all of them?"

"I think so." Maggie shined the flashlight around as much as possible in the confined space. "Oh…"

"What's wrong?"

"I think…I think there's one or two that didn't survive."

"Damn," Brad murmured. "Can you…do you think you can pass them out? We'll take them to the house."

"Of course." Her pants were soaked through, and her legs were numb. Well, except for the jagged rock stabbing above her kneecap. Maybe numb wasn't so bad? She stretched as far as she could—then she stretched a little bit more until her hand closed around one of the unmoving kittens.

She wriggled out of the log and climbed to her feet, carefully cradling the two tiny, blue-tinged bodies in her hands. "Come on. There's nothing more we can do here."

He made a noncommittal sort of noise and trudged toward the house. Hollyn met them at the edge of the yard. She grabbed the carrier from Brad and the two babies from Maggie and jogged to the house with them.

Brad looked paler by the moment. Maggie wrapped an arm around his waist to help him inside.

"I really am sorry about last night," he told her.

"Let's not worry about that right now. We need to get you warm and dry."

****

Elsie met them at the kitchen door. She helped peel off wet jackets and shoes while Maggie kept Brad balanced. He leaned heavily on her shoulder—probably more than he was aware of.

"The kittens—" Brad began.

"Your sister has the kittens in hand," Elsie assured him. "I set up a table in the dining room and unboxed the new incubator. I had to do something besides pace a groove in the floor waiting for you to check in."

Brad winced. "Sorry."

Elsie *hmphed*, but there was no real bite. She hung up their jackets, then spread an old towel underneath to catch the drips. "Go dry off before you catch cold."

"I've got him," Maggie replied. "Can you heat up

tea or maybe soup?"

"Certainly. Maybe a round of grilled cheese sandwiches, after everyone is settled?"

"That would be amazing." Maggie eyed Brad critically. "Okay. How long were you outside?"

He tried to smother a cough into clearing his throat. The attempt was fairly unconvincing. "Not sure."

She rolled her eyes.

"Hours," Elsie supplied.

"When's the last time you ate?"

"Sometime last night?"

"Drank?"

"He had a cup of coffee right before he went out." Elsie passed her a bottle of water and a sports drink.

Maggie shoved the water bottle into his hands. "Drink."

"I was a little busy."

"You're about to keel over. Drink."

He took a few gulps, then made a face. "Blech. Needs sugar and caffeine."

Maggie reclaimed the water bottle and handed him the sports drink.

"I meant coffee." He eyed the fluorescent liquid with distaste. "I hate this stuff."

"Yeah…funny thing about this stuff. It only tastes gross when you don't need it. If your electrolytes are screwed up, it goes down just fine."

She glared at him until he raised the bottle to his lips—and chugged most of the bright blue glop in one go.

"See?"

"All right, all right…you guys win."

"We always do," Elsie told him. "Now, shoo.

You're dripping on my nice clean floor."

"Yes, ma'am."

Maggie helped Brad squelch up the stairs. He automatically tried to detour into Miss Kitty's room.

"Uh-uh. Everyone else can look after the kittens just this once. You're a mess, and borderline hypothermic. Shower off the mud, then fill the tub and soak. Tell me where to find your clean clothes."

He flushed. "Uh…room at the top of the stairs. There's a bunch of clean laundry on the chair."

She steered him into the bathroom and started the shower. "Let the water warm up."

He fumbled with his wet clothes. "The towels are—"

"In the linen closet. I know."

She stepped out and selected three fluffy dry towels from the closet. When she returned to the bathroom, Brad hadn't made much headway.

"Do you need help?"

He raised an eyebrow at that, and she felt a blush creep up her neck.

"I'm a paramedic," she reminded him. "There's nothing you've got that I haven't seen before. And your hands are freezing."

"I can manage," he mumbled, cheeks blazing.

"Okay. I'll go get you a pair of clean pjs."

"You don't have to—"

"Look, if we're ever going to sit down and talk about last night, first you have to be healthy. Right now, that means getting warm. So you're going to get in the shower, and I'm going to find you something dry to wear. Don't argue with me because I'll win…and Elsie and Hollyn will back me up."

"You know we will," Hollyn assured him from the hallway.

"No fair ganging up on me," Brad croaked. He cleared his throat, obviously trying to repress another cough.

"I've been ganging up on you my whole life."

Maggie edged into the hallway, and Hollyn pressed a change of clothes and two more towels into her hands.

"You're a mess too. Go on and take a shower in the other bathroom. I'll brave my brother's laundry pile."

"How are they doing?" Brad asked through the closed door.

"Brad, so help me, will you get yourself in the shower? In case you've forgotten, I'm an actual licensed professional veterinarian. Plus, I've got Elsie. So I think we can manage."

"But—"

"Brad," both women chorused.

There was muffled profanity, and the shower curtain rattled.

"How are they doing?" Maggie murmured.

Hollyn sighed. "The ones who were moving when you found them are hanging on. They're in the incubator. Once they're at a safe temperature, I can feed them. The other two were already gone."

"I was afraid of that, but Brad wanted to try."

"My brother still believes in miracles. It's one of his more endearing traits." Hollyn gave Maggie a little shove in the direction of the other bathroom. "Go on. Get cleaned up. And hey—thanks for dragging Brad in out of the rain."

"My pleasure," Maggie assured her.

"You two…?"

"We'll talk about it once we're sure he doesn't have pneumonia. I promise."

"Okay."

Chapter Seventeen

"Brad? Are you alive in there?" Hollyn called through the closed door.

Brad startled—he'd been on the verge of dozing off in the tub. Probably not the best survival strategy. Then again, his impending chat with Maggie wasn't looking too appealing, either. Groaning, he hauled himself out of the tub and toweled off. Hollyn had left him sweats, a T-shirt, thick socks, and his slippers.

Elsie waited in the hallway, laundry basket in hand.

"Give me your wet clothes," she instructed him crisply.

"I'll toss them in the wash tomorrow."

"No, I'll wash your clothes and Maggie's tonight, so the mud doesn't set in."

"You only wash cat laundry."

"And tonight, I'm washing yours. Don't get used to it."

"What time is it, anyway?" Brad wondered. "It must be—"

"I'm staying."

"We're all staying," Hollyn added. "You're a mess, and we're not leaving you alone with two litters of fragile babies. So take yourself downstairs and eat some hot soup and for the love of God, talk to Maggie. We've got this."

A bit bemused, he wandered downstairs. Maggie sat

at the kitchen counter, eating a bowl of soup with one hand and shielding said bowl from Nixie with the other. He and Se prowled hopefully around the base of the island. Maggie wore some of his sister's clothes, her hair was damp from the shower, and she was still the most beautiful thing he'd ever seen.

"Hey," he mumbled.

She looked at him with a small smile. "Hey."

"I'm sorry," they both said at the same time.

"Ladies first."

"I'll talk, if you sit and have a hot drink," Maggie replied.

"Deal."

"There are cinnamon buns in the oven, too."

Maggie waited while he assembled two mugs of cocoa and set one in front of her. Then, he hopped onto the stool next to her and wrapped his hands around his own mug.

She blew on her drink, then took a long sip before speaking. "Look…I overreacted last night. I said things I shouldn't have."

"Last night was important, and I disappointed you."

"Not intentionally, and not…carelessly. What you do is important, and I didn't respect that enough."

"This is my life," he murmured into his cup. "I really want you in it, too, but my world will always come to a screeching halt for an animal emergency."

"Just like mine when the alarm bell rings."

"I can't change who I am."

"I don't want you to change. I like you the way you are."

He raised an eyebrow at that.

"Okay…maybe a little less stubborn? At least as far

as accepting help sometimes?"

Brad cracked a tired grin. "Deal. And I really am sorry about last night."

"Fresh start, okay?" Maggie leaned in closer and touched his face lightly. "You're flushed. Are you feeling all right?"

"I feel like I was outside getting rained on all day."

"Mm-hm. I think you need to take a couple of aspirin and go to bed."

"You're probably right," Brad admitted ruefully. "Right after I—" Maggie gave him a look. "—peek in on the kittens because I want to see them, even though I know Hollyn and Elsie are perfectly capable?" He muffled another cough.

Maggie slipped from her seat and stepped over in front of him. "I know that's a pretty huge concession from you."

Brad held out his arms, and she stepped into his embrace, sliding her arms around his waist. He held her close, resting his cheek on top of her head.

After a moment, she pulled away and took a good look at his face, then laid a hand on his cheek. "Okay. I think we need to get you into bed."

He waggled his eyebrows, which might have been more effective if his eyes weren't so glassy. She smacked his chest lightly.

"I mean it. You're wheezing. I know you're very well set up for cat meds. What do you have on hand for people? Aspirin? Acetaminophen? Anything for colds?"

"Maybe?"

She shook her head. "I'll ask Hollyn. Drink that and eat a bowl of soup and a bun."

"I'm not really—"

She looked over her shoulder.

"Right. Soup and a bun."

****

Brad woke blearily, groping around for another tissue. He succeeded in knocking the box to the floor. Wind howled around the eaves and rain lashed the windows. He fumbled for his phone and checked the time.

No. Oh, nonono.

He'd slept straight past midnight and beyond. They had two litters of tiny fragile babies in-house and he hadn't stirred in hours. He swung his legs over the side of the bed and staggered to his feet—or tried to. One foot came down on a fishy toy that sprang to life, flopping and making appalling noises.

Jolted wide awake, he groped around for his slippers, then gave up and went barefoot, hopping across the chilly floor. He hobbled down the narrow stairs rather faster than was safe. Why the hell hadn't someone woken him? The kittens were so delicate at this stage. They couldn't go too long between bottles. Every gram counted when they were so tiny. He couldn't—absolutely couldn't—lose any more.

The hinges creaked alarmingly when he pushed the door open, but no one broke the stillness to yell at him. The guest room door was nudged slightly open, probably by Nixie. Hollyn hadn't even bothered with hers. He followed the dim glow of nightlights to the new babies' room, wheezing a little from the exertion. If he angled his face to the glass properly, he could see inside the nest. Miss Kitty was curled around her brood, peaceful as a Madonna in a Christmas crêche. A bright yellow sticky note covered in Hollyn's scrawl stuck to the window.

2 a.m. They are fine Brad. Get your butt back to bed.

He pushed off the doorframe and headed downstairs, sidestepping a suspicious shadow on the landing. The kitchen was half lit, but empty. The dull hum of the dryer mingled with the clatter of rain against the windows. Hollyn must have chucked in another load of wash the last time she checked on the kittens. The kibble bowl was overturned, its contents scattered across the floor. Directions and accouterments for mixing kitten formula littered the countertop.

He poked his head into the living room and saw Mocha sleeping in a pile of rumpled bedding on the sofa. The dining room was brightly lit, and he heard a woman's voice murmuring sleepy nonsense. He crossed the room and leaned against the doorframe to catch his breath.

It wasn't Hollyn or Elsie, but Maggie at the table with the kittens. She wore one of Hollyn's ratty old T-shirts and sported a marvelous case of bedhead. A tiny tabby wriggled in her hands, slurping the contents of an equally tiny bottle.

"How're you doing?" he rasped. His throat felt like it was lined with razor blades—usually the first harbinger of the plague. *Swell.*

"We're doing fine," she assured him.

He slipped farther into the room and saw neatly printed instructions and reference photos pinned to the wall. A tablet leaned on a stand with a bottle-feeding tutorial made by a popular west coast rescuer paused on the screen.

A small smirk flirted with Maggie's lips as if she was reading his mind. "Plus, there's an actual vet upstairs. We're fine."

His fingers itched to check the weight chart, but he could see he really didn't need to. His team had the situation perfectly in hand, right down to the package of the super-soft toilet paper he bought especially for the kittens, and evidence Maggie was dealing with that "end" of things as well. She set the tabby in the incubator where the siblings wriggled closer into the cuddle puddle on a wooly lamb cushion.

She selected the tiny cow kitty and placed them on the scale, noting their weight. The kitten uttered a squeaky protest, and Maggie murmured some nonsense under her breath, guiding them to the bottle. She flickered a glance in his direction.

"How're you feeling?"

"Superfluous."

"I think the word you're looking for is 'sick.' And what're you doing wandering around with bare feet?"

"I was in a rush, and I couldn't find my slippers."

She raised an eyebrow at him. "And you were in a rush because?"

He huffed out a laugh. "Because I'm an idiot."

"You are. Now grab a drink and a couple more aspirin and go back to bed. We've got this."

Brad grinned wearily. "Yeah, you do." He shuffled to the kitchen. His babies—and his heart—were in good hands.

****

The next time he woke, the house was eerily quiet. And dark. There was no glow of electronic devices and no hum of a radio or TV. The bedside lamp didn't switch on. He shivered despite the covers. This was not good. He fumbled in the drawer of his nightstand for a flashlight, sending a couple of books clattering onto the floor in the process. Miracle of miracles, the batteries were still good.

It sounded like the storm had passed, but not much light seeped through the curtains. He gave up trying to find his slippers and stuffed his feet into a pair of thick socks. He snagged a heavy sweater off the bedpost. The steps creaked beneath his feet, and he made out voices from the hallway. He opened the door carefully and stepped out.

A heavy-duty flashlight on top of the bookcase cast witchy Maggie- and Elsie-shaped shadows on the walls.

Maggie turned toward him, worry mingled with the smile on her face. "Should you be out of bed?" She laid a hand on his forehead, then shifted to his cheek. "You feel feverish."

He was a mess, and his face was all stubbly, but her hand was so soft and warm. "Why's the house so cold?" he croaked.

"There're trees and branches down all over town. No power."

His sluggish brain took longer than normal to process that. "The babies—"

"Miss Kitty can take care of her brood—" Elsie said. "—And I can always tuck a hand warmer under their blankets."

"But the new babies—"

Maggie squeezed his shoulder. "The Tylers are helping Hollyn clean off the car. We'll take them to her office. If there's no power there, the police station has a generator."

He realized she was wearing her uniform. "You have to go in?"

"Yeah. The aftermath of this sort of thing spawns as

many accidents as the actual storm. Sometimes even more. People who have no business being anywhere near power tools mess with chainsaws or throw their backs out bailing water. And don't get me started on idiots with gas cans."

He snuffled and cleared his throat. "Be careful."

"I will. Ted and I are on loan to Chief Parker for the day, so I won't be far." She leaned up and pressed a kiss to his jaw. "I don't suppose there's any use telling you to go back to bed?"

He opened his mouth to assure her he would, but she raised an eyebrow, and he chuckled ruefully. Or tried to. It came out more as a tired wheeze.

"What if I promise to stay on the couch?"

"I'll make sure he does," Elsie assured her.

"Maggie," Hollyn yelled from downstairs.

"On my way."

"Take those sandwiches I wrapped up for you," Elsie reminded her.

"I will. I'll check in when I can."

Brad trailed down the stairs after them. The view from the front door was uninspiring, to say the least. Broken tree limbs littered the street and sidewalks. Formerly bagged leaves, trash, and recycling had blown into untidy heaps, clogging the gutters and storm drains. Nate consoled little Mandy for the loss of their jack-o-lanterns blown and smashed all over the yard. The Rogers boys ranged the neighborhood, collecting pieces of their shattered display. Wait—kids? Wasn't it Monday?

"The schools are closed," Elsie said, as if reading his mind. "No power." She passed Maggie a thermal bag.

"We're not too sure about the bus routes, either"

Maggie added, looping the bag over her shoulder. "Chief Parker and the principals decided it was safer not to open." She jostled his arm. "Hey…we'll be fine in the SUV, and if we come to anything unsafe to drive through, I have friends with four-by-fours I can call. We'll get them someplace warm and safe. I promise."

"Maggie," Hollyn bellowed from the driveway.

"Coming," she yelled over her shoulder. She stooped and picked up Nixie and pressed her into Brad's arms. "We'll be fine. Now get in out of the draft."

Chapter Eighteen

Maggie didn't realize how deeply Carson Mills had wormed its way into her heart until she saw the damage from the storm. She sat in the back seat, keeping a careful grip on the incubator and its precious cargo.

Downed utility poles and fallen trees were commonplace in her line of work. The shattered remnants of the treehouse she passed every day since she moved here? Not so much. The pond at the golf course had expanded past the newly repaired fence. Well, at least the rotten geese were happy.

"I feel so bad for the kids," she blurted. "I know there are more important things, but...all those Halloween events everyone's been talking about all month."

Hollyn kept her eyes on the road. "I know. It sucks. We'll make things work somehow. We always do."

"How? There's so much damage."

"The haunted house, dance, and kids' carnival are held in the school gyms, so all that stuff should be fine."

"But what about power?"

Hollyn was silent for a moment as she concentrated on skirting an enormous puddle. "About ten years ago, there was a freak October snowstorm. A lot of trees still had their leaves, and the snow was heavy and wet. Trees came down all over town and power was out for days. Everything had to be canceled, and the mayor prohibited trick or treating for safety reasons. So we had Halloween two weeks later." She grinned. "Kids had to wear coats and mittens over their costumes and a lot of the candy had Christmas wrappers, but they didn't care." She slowed to a stop at a darkened traffic signal.

Maggie craned her neck to see the street sign. The green and white paint was faded beyond recognition. "What're these streets?" she asked, mid-text.

"Route 3 and Orchard Road." Hollyn eased down on the gas pedal. "Then the following year, we were hit with the edges of a monster fall storm."

"This far inland?"

Hollyn nodded. "Yeah. That thing was a movie-grade disaster. We were close enough to score damage, but far enough away we didn't qualify for help from the government. They were pouring all their resources into opening the airports and thruways so they could get supplies to the rest of the state. That year it was Thanksgiving by the time we could do anything for the kids."

They passed a family trying to shift large sections of fallen fence. Maggie sent another text—that was an accident waiting to happen.

"Anyway, the mayor finally obtained a disaster recovery grant and the electricity in the center of town was upgraded. We have generators for the main buildings, too, so we can activate shelters and warming stations if we need them."

Property damage seemed lighter on Main Street—a few loose awnings, three trash cans rolling around and a broken window or two. The wonderful autumn decorations were a different story. Waterlogged cornstalks, bedraggled ribbons, and smashed pumpkins mingled with masses of wet leaves, slicking the pavement. The street in front of town hall was coned off for emergency vehicles. Maggie spotted fire department and power company vehicles, the DPW truck, and her ambulance, but not her wayward partner.

Hollyn double parked next to a tractor and a couple of heavy-duty pickups from the orchard. Maggie secured the incubator with a seat belt and slid out, mindful of her footing on the slimy fallen leaves.

Hollyn slung an arm over the back of the seat and stared at her. "So, are you and my brother okay?"

Maggie smiled. "Yeah, I think we are."

"Good. Be careful."

"I will." Maggie shut the door and stepped away. She climbed the wet marble steps with a death grip on the railing and followed the babble of voices to a large event room. Halloween props and cases of candy and carnival prizes were pushed aside to accommodate a makeshift command center. Chief Parker and Mayor Roman had a large map of the town spread on a folding banquet table. A quick glance revealed Ted next to— what else?—the hastily assembled snack table.

Chief Parker looked up from comparing a written list to sticky dots on the map. "Maggie, thanks for your texts. We're adding that information. Carson Circle is okay, except for the power?"

"Yes, sir. A lot of small branches and a few shingles, and someone's hammock wrapped around a tree, but nothing major."

He scanned the room and nodded, seemingly satisfied everyone was present, then rapped his knuckles on the table. "Okay, folks. We were lucky this time. Most of the storm activity was overnight, so we only had one vehicular incident. The rest looks like property damage and power outages. My deputies are identifying hot spots and—"

He broke off as the First Lady's voice rose irritably. "Sir, for the sixth time, I'm sorry you can't find your dog but—"

"May I have the phone, Ms. Roman?" He held out his hand. "Thank you." He raised the phone to his ear. "Mr. Carson, I am very sorry your dog escaped from the yard you've been instructed to fence in multiple times. The town is currently in a state of emergency. If you harass any member of my team again, I'll have you arrested. Have a nice day." He ended the call and passed the phone back. "Ma'am." He nodded politely. "Hang up on him if he calls again. Now then…Maggie and Ted, can you run out to Jeff and Edith Cox's place for a wellness check? They're in their eighties and she's diabetic."

"Insulin?" Ted asked. As usual, when he was working, there was no trace of the happy-go-lucky snack thief.

The chief consulted his notes "She's got enough on hand, but they don't have power, so take them a couple of bags of ice for their fridge, would you please? You can grab some from the diner. Mitch, can you please take your crew to Maple Court? One of the big trees on the corner is down blocking the road."

Mitch settled his Bobbins and Apples cap on his head. "Aw, that's a shame. Those were gorgeous."

"If we can get a team clearing the gutters and storm drains, that would be great. Rakes and push brooms are downstairs in the basement. Buddy system, everyone. Please let us know of anything you see that ought to be on the map. Tyler Automotive is standing by to assist with any disabled vehicles. Do not attempt to drive through standing water. Pete?" he turned to a power company rep.

"Remember, everyone—if you see any electrical equipment down, do not approach. Even if it looks dead, call in your location and we'll make sure."

Mayor Roman stood. "I want to thank all of you for your help. Anyone not employed by the town or county, please be sure to pick up a safety vest and a voucher. We have tabs running at Tyler's, the hardware store, and the diner. Everyone please grab some water and stay safe."

****

Ted drove back from the Coxes' while Maggie jotted down notes about damage, occasionally texting the command center if something appeared to be a clear and present danger. Families were out in full force, clearing yards and checking on elderly neighbors.

"This must be where the truck went off the road last night," Ted muttered. "Kelsey said it was nasty. They had to wait for a break in the storm to airlift the driver."

Maggie saw the tire marks and churned-up grass at the side of the road. "Wait—what's that?"

"Where?"

"There, under the tree." She pointed to a pale shape huddled at the base of a towering pine.

****

Hollyn's clinic occupied part of a two-story red brick plaza a couple of blocks away from town hall. Beveled tan brickwork outlined the doors and windows and the overhang of the roof. Her neighbors included a dentist and optometrist. The sidewalk trees had lost their leaves and a few branches, and the mums in the concrete planters were blown flat, but that seemed to be the extent of the damage.

Maggie's feet skidded on wet leaves when she hopped down. "Looks like she has power."

Ted swung open the back door. "This place just looks like the set from a classic sitcom on the outside. The building's pretty new. It was designed to handle all sorts of tech and has plenty of backups."

"Then how come the sign on the pharmacy says 'established 1927?' "

" 'Cuz it's a family business, and the latest generation recognized the necessity of reliable high-speed internet and battery backups."

Lights glowed from the windows and a puff of warm air gusted out when Hollyn came outside to meet the ambulance, pulling on a pair of latex exam gloves. "I knew this was gonna happen someday."

Maggie and Ted carefully unloaded the gurney containing a motionless Cuthbert strapped to a backboard.

"We think he was hit by a truck last night," Maggie told her. "He was tossed to the side of the road. It was pitch dark and pouring rain when the call came in. He would have been invisible to the first responders."

"I never liked the stupid mutt, but I'm sorry it came to this." Ted grunted with effort as they wrestled the gurney over the threshold.

"It's not his fault," Hollyn replied. "It never was."

"What do you think?" Maggie asked.

Hollyn surveyed the dog's still form and sighed. "Well, I'm pretty sure he'll lose that leg. Technically, I need permission to treat him. That'll be a fun call."

Ted touched her arm lightly. "You'll do your best. I

have faith in you, Doc."

Hollyn looked up from her patient briefly and favored him with a crooked little smile.

Maggie repressed a smirk. "How're the babies?"

"They're…" Hollyn glanced at her watch. "Crud. They're due for a feeding. Any chance you two could spare a few minutes?"

Ted shrugged. "We're due for a lunch break. I always wanted to see those cute little buggers up close."

"Keep telling yourself that when we get to part two of the feeding process."

****

Brad blinked open gummy eyes. He felt…well, not better. Slightly less cruddy? Yeah, he'd go with that. He tried to move without much success—the blanket was pinned down by two warm furry weights. He shoved himself up on his elbows, disrupting Mocha and Nixie. At least this time the room wasn't spinning. Much. The house had the empty stillness that spoke of no electricity running through its veins.

Pill bottles, tissue boxes, and empty beverage containers littered the coffee table. Used tissues scattered across the floor from a small tipped-over wastebasket. *Gross. Thanks, Nixie.* Light footsteps creaked on the steps—Elsie. Hollyn couldn't move quietly if she tried. And she usually didn't.

There seemed to be plenty of activity outside, however. He stood and shuffled toward the front window. *I have to get out there soon. I hafta rake up all those leaves and branches and check the gutters—*

"Brad MacKenzie, what are you doing up?" Elsie balanced a laundry basket on one hip. One of his hoodies swamped her slight frame.

He gestured vaguely at the window. "I have to get dressed and clean up."

"Clean up what, exactly?"

"The leaves and…stuff…"

"Think again." She set down her basket and walked with him to the window. She parted the curtains enough to see outside.

Nate and one of the Rogers boys saw them and waved. They'd almost finished bagging the last of the leaves from the lawn. Nate's daughter Mandy carefully removed leaves from the garden statues and planters, filling her own little bag.

"Folks heard you were sick and wanted to help."

He blinked. "How long was I asleep?" From his vantage point, it looked like maybe half the block had been set to rights. Leaves were bagged or raked into neat piles. Broken branches were bundled together and stacked on the curb. Mr. Carson's yard was conspicuously untouched.

Elsie snorted. "Not long enough, from the sound of you. Why don't you freshen up a little while I tidy the living room?"

He scrubbed a hand through his hair, which did nothing to improve its appearance. "I should check on the cats."

Elsie leveled a stare that had been known to quail the hearts of champion football players back in the day.

"Except I don't have to because you've already taken care of everything?"

She nodded.

"What about the forest babies?"

"Your sister is keeping them with her. The clinic has power, and she needs to stay in town anyway."

Brad glanced out the window again. "I'm amazed Mr. Carson isn't out there taking notes to register complaints about the mess."

Elsie sighed. "He has other things to worry about right now. Cuthbert got loose the night of the storm and was hit by a truck. The rescue workers didn't see him in the downpour. Maggie and her partner found him this morning."

"Is he—?"

"Your sister managed to save him. He's a tripod, but he's alive."

Brad's lips thinned. *That beautiful animal lost a leg because his owner was...*

As usual, Elsie seemed to sense his thoughts. "Your sister saved him, after he'd been lying outside in the storm all night. If you've ever wondered how good she is—"

"I don't need to wonder. I never have."

"It wouldn't hurt for you to tell her so occasionally. Anyway, Maggie's partner Ted assisted with the surgery. He's going to stay at the clinic tonight in case she needs help."

"At the clinic, huh? Do I need to prepare a shovel speech?"

Elsie set her hands on her hips and eyed him. "Yes, dear, because you look so terribly formidable right now."

He sniffled and tried to stand straighter.

"You need to trust your sister. She's a grown woman. I'm sure Ted is a very nice guy."

He probably was, or Maggie wouldn't tolerate him, but that didn't mean he couldn't have a little fun with the situation.

"Anyway, Chief Parker will drop Maggie off, then

take me home in one of the four-by-fours. Do you mind if I leave my car here?"

"Of course not. I don't want you driving in this mess."

She raised an eyebrow at that. "I've been driving since before you were born. Go get cleaned up. Shoo." She waved her hands at him.

****

Washing in cold water in a cold bathroom by the light of a battery-powered lantern wasn't a particularly enjoyable endeavor, so Brad didn't prolong the process any more than necessary. He pulled a fresh T-shirt over his head and combed his hair. *Eh, good enough. It's not like there's anyone to see me.*

He shone his light into each of the cat rooms. The boxes were scooped, food and water dishes full, and the occupants went about their business, doing important cat things. The flashlight beam made spooky shadows of the cardboard haunted houses in each room. He headed downstairs, wincing as he stepped on a squeaky toy.

Maggie straightened from fluffing the pillows and blankets on the sofa. "Hey. I thought I'd stay and help keep an eye on things tonight. If that's okay?"

He cleared his throat—twice, and didn't that sound gross? "Always."

"Do you think Mocha minds sharing his couch again?"

He shrugged slightly. "Depends. Is there room for both of us?"

She smiled at him. "Always."

"I heard about today." He spotted a barf on the rug and backtracked for cleaner and paper towels.

"We think we cleared most of the dangerous debris."

Maggie kept talking as he cleaned the spot and deposited the mess in the trash. Yay for nasal congestion—returned cat food was hardly a favorite fragrance.

"Power company guy is hopeful the whole town'll be back online in the next twenty-four hours. Did the dry ice truck get here?"

He detoured and checked the fridge. "I don't think so." There was no light, of course, but the interior was vaguely cool. If the power came back in the next couple of hours the contents might be okay. He shooed Nixie out of the way and shut the door.

"The mayor decided to hold off on the schools until Wednesday—make sure the roads are clear and give folks a chance to shower, wash clothes, and cook. Which reminds me—I have a care package from the diner. Come eat while the food's warm."

He eased into the corner of the L-shaped sectional and Maggie curled up beside him. Mocha hopped up between them and made biscuits on a blanket, purring like an outboard motor. Maggie reached over him and handed Brad a sandwich and a go cup of coffee—the first warm thing he'd ingested all day.

"Tell me about your adventures."

Maggie waved a hand vaguely while she chewed and swallowed. "Mostly we got lucky. We did wellness checks for elderly folks and people with known disabilities. We prevented a couple of idiots from barbecuing themselves."

"Dare I ask?"

"A tree came down on top of their car. They thought it would be a great idea to set the tree on fire so it would fall apart. I think they got the idea from a dumb internet video."

He picked his way through a haze of cold medicine. "They wanted to set a fire...on top of a car...which contains gasoline and oil?"

She nodded, rolling her eyes. "They had a garden hose nearby."

"A garden hose." Brad groaned and rolled his head against the back of the couch.

"Luckily we arrived before they could dowse everything with gas and convinced them to wait for the crew from the orchard, who know how to move trees safely. Buncha idiots." She took a long swallow of coffee. "Then...well, you've probably heard this part by now. We found Cuthbert on the side of the road."

"I heard. We've been telling Mr. Carson for years something like this was going to happen. I just wish Cuthbert wasn't the one to pay the price."

"Mayor Roman and Chief Parker went to town on him this time. He has thirty days to build a proper fence and have Cuthbert trained, or animal control will seize the dog and put him up for adoption."

"That might be best for all concerned."

Maggie slumped against him. "It's not that easy. He looked so...broken when he came into the clinic. I think under his nonsense, Mr. Carson is really very lonely."

"If he is, it's his own fault. Elsie says he's been like this for as long as she can remember. There's only so many times people get their hands slapped before they stop reaching out to someone."

Maggie collected the detritus of their meal. "Want anything from the kitchen?"

"No, thanks." He heard her bustling around checking locks, and then she settled into the corner of the couch with him. "Sure you want to be this close?"

"Since the alternative is having your feet in my face, I'll take my chances."

"We're the only ones here. You could take one of the upstairs rooms and sleep in a real bed."

She cocked her head to one side. "Are you trying to get rid of me?"

"Never."

"Well, then." She snuggled into his shoulder and dragged a couple of throws from the back of the couch.

Chapter Nineteen

A low, rumbling hum woke Maggie. *Furnace? Hot water heater? Both, maybe?* Lights flickered on and assorted small appliances hummed to life.

Something tugged at her hair. She shifted around and saw Nixie happily ensconced on their shared pile of pillows, grooming her curls. She shoved herself up on one elbow, pushing a few stray locks of hair out of her eyes and reclaiming the rest from Nixie, earning a disgruntled meow. Her movements disturbed He and Se, who stretched and added to the cacophony of meows.

The pile of blankets on the other side of the sectional shifted and snuffled. Mocha took that to mean breakfast was forthcoming and stood on Brad's chest.

He emitted a sound somewhere between a grunt and a gasp and pushed Mocha aside. "Is the power back?"

"Seems like it. Did you think to unplug the computers?"

Brad made a vaguely affirmative noise and fumbled for his phone to check the time. He peered owlishly at the blank screen for a few seconds. "Nuts."

"Try mine. I charged it any time I was near an outlet yesterday."

Brad touched the screen and Maggie's phone sprang to life. He grinned at the lock screen—a picture of Cosmos and Nebula. "It is indeed Tuesday morning. Very, very early Tuesday morning." He sat all the way up, scrubbing a hand over his face. "I should check the basement."

Maggie slid out of the nest of blankets and shivered. "Let me—"

"I know where everything is, and I can tell what's normal quicker than you. I won't linger down there. Promise."

"Put something on your feet." She bent to grab her shoes and a cat hopped on her back and started making biscuits. "You know, I'm pretty sure Elsie filled your bowls before she left."

Brad scooped up Nixie so she could stand. "Oh, she did, but you're part of the team. Your life is now dedicated to feeding the monsters and dangling toys."

"There are worse things. I'll check the kitchen."

"Open the fridge at your own risk."

She shuddered. "I don't even wanna think about mine."

****

By the time Brad ascertained the heat and hot water were behaving themselves, and there wasn't water anyplace it didn't belong, a savory scent emanated from the kitchen. He turned the thermostat up a couple degrees and followed his nose.

Maggie glanced over her shoulder from the pot she was stirring. "The dry ice truck didn't make it this far, and I don't trust the milk in your fridge, so I found a can of chicken soup."

"Smells great."

"You can smell this? Good."

"Yeah." He sniffed. "My sinuses"—he cleared his throat "—seem to have...sorry. Not a nice topic over breakfast."

"Hello? Paramedic, remember? Grab yourself a bowl—I think this is almost done. I figured we could both do with something hot."

Brad grabbed a couple of bowls and spoons, dodging He and Se. He nudged Nixie off the counter so he could set the dishes down. "All right, all right—I'll feed you." He popped the tops off a couple cans of food and grimaced—he could have done without stinky fish smell, thanks very much. Mocha strolled in and shouldered the others aside disdainfully. "There's four dishes, you know, and they've all got the same thing in them."

"You know logic doesn't work on cats. Come and eat."

He slid onto one of the barstools and stirred his soup. He blew on it, then slurped a big spoonful. The heat traveled down his throat and warmed him. "This is amazing."

"This is from a can." But her cheeks blushed pink all the same.

They ate in companionable silence for the next few moments, then he recollected something. "So…tell me about this partner of yours."

Maggie sipped another spoonful of soup, then patted her lips with a paper towel. "What, Ted?"

"If he's the one who spent the night in my sister's clinic, then yeah."

"Ted." She covered her mouth, snorting with laughter. "Ted?"

"Yeah. Elsie said—"

"You know Hollyn has a really big dog in her clinic, right? One who just lost a leg? And she's not a comic book superhero who can magically lift all things."

"Okay, but—"

"Would you rather your sister was dealing with that alone?"

"Well, when you put it like that…"

Maggie scrunched her face and tried to control her chortles. "Okay, look…Ted's a great guy. He's a first-rate medic and one of the most dependable people I know. But he also thinks donuts are one of the major food groups."

Brad tipped his bowl to get the last bit of soup. "So does Hollyn, as it happens."

"So what's the problem?"

"She's my kid sister."

"Um, you know she's not a kid anymore, right? She's an actual grown-up professional?"

He winced. "She'll always be my kid sister."

Maggie turned to him and laid a hand on his arm. "Look, Ted's a goofball, but his heart's in the right place. He'd never hurt her. And honestly, he's there to help her schlep Cuthbert. And if you must know, I'm pretty sure he's sleeping on the couch in her waiting room."

Brad huffed out a laugh. "You're right. Of course you are."

She gathered the empty dishes and placed them in the sink. "Mind you, a little adult interaction wouldn't hurt either of them."

Brad whipped around on his stool at the word "adult."

"That's not what I meant, and you know it." Maggie tossed a dish towel printed with black cats at him. She glanced at the clock. "I should head home. I need a shower before work, and I want to check my kitchen."

He walked her to the door, scooping up Nixie on the

way so she couldn't resume her grand tour of the neighborhood. "Thanks for staying last night."

She stretched up and kissed his cheek. "Any time."

Brad opened the door and saw Nate poised to knock.

"Hey, Brad, Maggie. I'm gonna climb up and take a look at your gutters."

"I can—"

"Nope, you can't. Cold meds and ladders don't mix. 'Sides, I can do it faster and safer, and I know what I'm looking for. I'm checking everybody's. I'll let you know if I see anything that needs attention. You know I'd never gouge folks after a storm like this." He shot a dark look at the end of the circle. "Well, maybe someone, but you're not him. I'll just be a few minutes." He nodded at Maggie.

Brad watched Maggie until she passed the Tylers coming down the front steps and disappeared inside her own house, then shut the door. He went to his table and plugged in the computer and router. Outside, the neighborhood came to life. Nate's ladder thumped against the eaves and folks called greetings across the street. Marty Tyler's strident tones penetrated the closed windows, offering Mrs. Morgan a jumpstart. It was strange to hear people moving around without Cuthbert making a ruckus.

The house at the end of the circle loomed grim and silent. Leaves and broken branches littered the once-immaculate lawn. Mr. Carson didn't emerge to complain about the noise and activity in the neighborhood, or even to restore order to his precious yard.

****

Brad felt a bit more human after a shower and change of clothes. He heard a truck pull up and looked out the front window. The mail carrier shook her head "no" as she passed his gate. The Tylers were clearing broken branches from the apple tree and rehanging their Pride flag. People swapped tools and supplies as needed. The Rogers boys across the street laid out broken props on their lawn and tried to reassemble their yard scene. The archway they used for an entrance lay on its side and at least half of their meticulously carved foam tombstones were broken off at the base. *What a shame. They work so hard on their display every year.*

And little Mandy dragged a small trash bag down the street to old man Carson's. She started at the far corner of his lawn, determinedly scooping leaves into her bag. People stopped what they were doing to stare, expecting an imminent explosion. Nate slid down from his ladder and hurried after her.

Mandy shook her head at her dad and went right back to gathering leaves. After a few minutes, Nate walked to his yard and grabbed a rake. A few other folks drifted over to help, collecting broken branches, or raking leaves into neat piles. He let the curtain fall and headed back to his computer.

Wonders never cease.

The doorbell rang, and he and Nixie did the kitty tango to see who'd get to the door first. Nate stood on the doormat, looking rather sheepish. Brad nudged Nixie aside with his foot and stepped onto the porch.

"What's going on over there?"

Nate squirmed like a guilty schoolboy. "Mandy said she thought Mr. Carson would be sad his dog was run over. She wants to help."

"She's a sweet kid."

"I keep expecting him to come out screaming we're

trespassing, but he hasn't made a peep. Maybe she's right. I mean, if it was anyone else, we'd be happy to help." He scrubbed a hand through his hair. "Anyway, do you have any leaf bags or trash bags you can spare?"

"I think so. Check in the garage. Help yourself to whatever you need."

****

Brad settled in at his computer with a fresh cup of coffee and signed on to the Carson Mills Cares video conference. He took a long sip and wrinkled his nose. Despite what the ads claimed, powdered creamer—even the flavored kind—wasn't as good as milk. Still, it was caffeine. The computer finished doing its thing and thumbnails of familiar faces lined the screen.

"Brad, how are you feeling?" Mayor Roman asked.

He straightened in his chair and sniffed quietly, trying to look healthy. Ish. "Less plague-ridden, thanks."

"Good. And I hear there are kittens?"

"Two litters."

Marisol Roman leaned in next to her wife to share the screen. "You should do a calendar." Others murmured their agreement.

He paused with the coffee cup halfway to his mouth. That was definitely worth a thought. Lots of other rescues did them, very successfully.

Then Chief Parker signed on. "Is everyone here?"

"All present and accounted for." The mayor looked at the notes in her hands. "I suppose the first thing we want to settle is whether the schools will be open tomorrow?"

The head of the school board chimed in. "The buildings have power and most of the roads are clear for buses. Maple Court and a few other neighborhoods might need to walk their kids to the main road for pickup, but I think we're agreed, it's safer to have the kids in the schools."

Chief Parker cleared his throat. "On the topic of safety, I'd like to talk about Halloween. Obviously, we're trying to restore everything as quickly as possible, but realistically, we have wires and trees down, and clean up's going to take some time. There're places where trees came down and the roots busted though the pavement. I really don't like the idea of kids wandering around after dark. I think we ought to cancel trick or treat this year."

That idea was greeted with a lot of dismayed muttering. Mayor Roman raised a hand for silence. "Folks—folks—I get it. No one wants to disappoint their kids, but we have to think of their safety first. A lot of the houses that go all out had their decorations damaged by the storm. We don't need anyone having a house fire from a compromised extension cord or light fixture." She settled her glasses on her nose. "What I'm proposing is to extend the festivities already planned for the weekend. What if we ask folks to donate whatever goodies they have on hand, and kids can trick or treat around town square?"

"Tack it onto the Ragamuffin Parade on Saturday?" Charlie from the diner asked.

A discussion ensued about the pros and cons of disrupting shopping and parking and heaven knew what else.

Brad leaned his head on his hand. He tried to stay focused, but the voices faded into a hum of white noise.

"Brad? Brad, you still with us?"

He jerked awake, his head slipping from his fist.

"Hmm? Um, sorry…cold meds…"

The mayor chuckled. "No worries. I was just asking; how would you feel about chaperoning a mixer at the middle school Saturday night?"

He scrubbed at his eyes. "Sorry…mixer?"

She smiled patiently. "Yes. At the middle school. The sound system and decorations are set up for the Harvest Ball Friday night. We'll just get another night's use out of everything. We figure between that and the haunted house at the high school, there should be enough to keep the bigger kids occupied. The mixer will run until eleven. We'd like younger people for chaperones, to keep the atmosphere fun."

"Oh…um…sure."

"Thanks, Brad." Her smile turned sly. "You should bring someone. It's a dance, after all."

Her wife leaned in. "Don't forget a costume."

Right. A costume. And a date. And a gym full of rowdy kids. *What the hell did I just agree to?*

Chapter Twenty

Maggie paused outside the door to Miss Kitty's room. Brad was propped against the wall, eyes shut, evidently napping. A blanket full of tiny puffballs covered his lap, also snoozing. Nearby, Miss Kitty chowed down on a heaping bowl of wet food. Despite her misadventures in the big scary outside world, she was thriving under The Clowder's unique brand of TLC. Her gray fur was clean, and she had a white shirtfront and paws which hadn't been obvious the day of her rescue. She didn't spare Maggie more than a glance when she tapped on the glass.

Brad blinked awake and smiled sleepily. She padded inside on sock feet and offered him an oversized travel mug.

"Here. Coffee with real milk." She slid the top open and passed the mug to him handle first.

He freed a hand for the mug. "I think I'm in love." His eyes slid closed again as he blissfully inhaled coffee.

Funny you should phrase it that way…

She blinked. He was still drinking. She poked him in the arm. "Hey—come up for air."

"Sorry. But…you know…coffee."

"Trucks should be able to get through tomorrow to restock the stores."

"Good. The less said about the powdered stuff, the better." He set his mug down, then glanced sidewise at her. "Sorry. First world problems. How was your day?"

"Not too bad. Most folks were too busy trying to clean up their property to get into mischief. Chief Parker's deputies had a field day with the few who did." She petted one of the babies with her fingertips. They opened their tiny pink mouth in a silent hiss. Miss Kitty didn't look up from her meal, so Maggie picked up the little ball of tabby striped fluff and cuddled them against her chest.

They're so warm...and so soft. I can see why Brad does this. It's so easy to fall in love with him...I mean them.

Her cheeks warmed, and she looked through her lashes to see Brad watching her with a knowing smile. She blew an errant curl out of her face.

Right. No time like the present.

"I was wondering—"

"Are you—" they both blurted at the same time, then dissolved into easy chuckles.

"Ladies first," he prompted.

"Um. I was wondering if you had plans for Saturday?" Wait—was that a flash of disappointment in his eyes? "They canceled trick or treat, because Chief Parker doesn't think it's safe for the kids to be wandering around after dark, and a bunch of us were asked to man a candy station in the town square Saturday afternoon. I just...I thought maybe..." Relief washed through her as Brad's face relaxed into a grin.

"I was gonna ask you the same thing. More or less. I was asked to chaperone a mixer at the middle school that night." He paused and sucked in a deep breath. "I know a middle school dance isn't the same as a fancy ball, and I know I can never make up for disappointing you, but I was hoping—"

She didn't wait for the rest of his stammered explanation. She leaned in and kissed him. His lips were so warm. The kitten in her hands uttered a tiny peep of protest, and Miss Kitty whipped her head up and leveled a glare in their direction.

"Sorry," they both mumbled.

Miss Kitty shot them another look, then returned to her food.

She leaned in and pressed another kiss to the corner of his mouth. "I should have asked first—how are you feeling? Are you up to a whole day of sugar-crazed kids?"

"A whole day with you? I think I'll survive."

"I guess we need costumes?"

Brad nodded.

"Good thing we've got three whole days to figure out the details."

****

The next afternoon, Maggie pulled into a parking space near Hollyn's clinic. She hopped out and tightened her grip on the cardboard drink caddy and takeout bag from the diner. *Thank God someone collected the wet leaves. The last thing I need is to come through the stupid storm in one piece only to fall and break my head on a clear sunny day.* Colors smudged and smeared the plate glass windows. It took a few minutes for her to recognize the remnants of black cats and ghosties. Kids' artwork, done in washable paint.

What a shame…

She bopped the button with her elbow, opening the door, and walked inside.

Hollyn looked up from the kitten she was tending at

her desk. "This is all your fault."

Maggie glanced involuntarily over her shoulder. Nope. No one else was behind her. "Huh?" She looked around for someplace safe to put the drinks.

"You and my brother. Everyone thinks you're *so* cute and *so* sweet and *so* perfect."

What the hell did I walk into now?

"I'm….sorry?"

Hollyn set the bottle aside and carefully patted the kitten's back to make her burp. "Your partner asked me to the Halloween dance," she finally blurted.

"Ted?"

Hollyn just glared as she set the baby in the incubator and selected another.

Maggie relaxed slightly and opened one of the drinks, setting the foam cup on the desk, hopefully beyond spill range. "You know Ted volunteers for all the Halloween events, right? It's how he gets his month's supply of free junk food."

"But this is a dance. And he asked me to go with him. Because you two are going and 'Who knows, it might be fun.' "

"Um. Okay. Well, for one thing, we're not 'going to the dance,' we're chaperones. It's a mixer, to keep the older kids occupied on Halloween night."

"But it's a dance," Hollyn hissed, still holding the kitten's bottle at the correct angle.

"And we're just there to make sure the kids stay in the gym where they belong and don't go creeping off behind the bleachers or whatever. Plus we get free snacks. No big deal."

"It's a *dance*. And I'm going with a *guy*—"

"Wait—so you mean you said yes? *To Ted*?"

Hollyn flushed as red as the antique fire engine. "Honestly, I think I just made startled goldfish noises."

"Look, the guy's been sleeping on your sofa." Which was standard waiting room issue and didn't actually look terribly comfy. "I think you've probably figured out he's not—I mean, he's a great guy but—oh, hell, he's *Ted*."

"Okay. I mean, I know it's not prom, and he's not a romantic hero from a movie—"

Maggie snorted with laughter.

"—but he's a guy and it's a dance. Shouldn't I...I dunno, at least try to look like a girl for once?"

Maggie set a slice of pie and a plastic fork beside Hollyn's cup. "Gimme the kitten and eat this. We'll figure everything out. We've got a couple of days."

"Right. 'Cuz there's such a great selection left by now." The bells on the door jingled, admitting a damp breeze and two firefighters. "Are you collecting for the trick or treat?" Hollyn asked. "I have a couple of rolls of stickers, but I sorta got into the candy."

"Nah...actually we're here to help. We heard you're housing a big dog and could use a hand moving him around?"

Maggie shook her head and mouthed "not me." "Hollyn, this is Kelsey and Matt from the station."

"Um. Wow. Thanks. I have Cuthbert who just became a tripod. He needs help to go outside and do his business. He's relearning how to walk and balance."

"Okay. Do you want us to carry him, or do you have a big towel or sheet we can use for a sling?"

"And a spare pooper scooper?"

****

Brad crept around the cluster of trucks clogging the

town square looking for a parking spot. DPW workers and volunteers had worked wonders clearing the debris from the storm. Now everyone pitched in, trying to make magic for the kids. Mitch and the crew from Bobbins and Apples unloaded fresh haybales on the green. The First Ladies discarded the battered and broken remains of the mums and replaced them with arrangements of jack-o-lanterns and fancy gourds.

He finally found a spot and hopped out, grabbing a couple of shopping bags from the back of the SUV.

"Brad!" Mayor Roman waved a grubby hand. "How are you feeling?"

"Better, thanks."

"Good. I'm glad to hear it. Most of the jack-o-lanterns for the carving contest were ruined."

"Aw…that's a shame."

"We're replacing them with whatever people can produce quickly. Can we prevail upon you to carve a couple of your wonderful cat-o-lanterns? We saved a few pumpkins for you."

He grinned. "Depends. Do I have to scoop out the guts?" That wasn't a deal breaker, but slimy pumpkin innards were his least favorite part of the holiday festivities.

Mitch shoved his hat back and wiped his forehead. "Nah. I had a batch already scooped. Carving station is over on the picnic tables."

"In that case, you're on."

"What've you got there?" the mayor asked, wiping her hands on her workshop apron.

"Contributions for the trick or treat. Stickers, pencils, and a couple bags of candy I managed to hide from my sister. Plus a batch of Elsie's chocolate chippers for the crew."

"We'll be sure to hide the cookies from Chief Parker until the rest of us get some." She winked and took the bags. "Mitch will find you a set of carving tools."

Brad looked around the square. A crew festooned the gazebo with ragged black cheesecloth "cobwebs" and strings of purple fairy lights. A batch of freshly carved jack-o-lanterns adorned the steps of the library. "This is gonna look really great."

"It usually does when this town comes together. I just hope—" Her eyes widened as she caught sight of something over Brad's shoulder.

He turned and saw Mr. Carson hobbling toward them. He had an old shoe box tucked under one arm.

Mayor Roman inhaled sharply and plastered a professional smile on her face. "Mr. Carson. What can we do for you today?"

The old man's craggy face flushed red. He thrust his box into the mayor's hands. "Here. For the trick or treat." He turned jerkily and stomped away, leaning on his cane.

"Thank you," she called belatedly.

Marisol Roman hurried over and wrapped an arm around her wife. "What is it?"

"I don't know." The mayor shook the box. "It's heavy. He said it was for the trick or treat." She lifted the lid almost fearfully.

Not that I blame her. Who knows what goes through that old man's mind. Still, he and the others crowded close to see.

"Pennies?" She showed her wife the box full of neatly rolled coins. "I don't think people have given out pennies for trick or treat since he was a kid."

"What on earth are we supposed to do with so many

pennies?"

She shrugged philosophically. "We'll think of something. I think this is the first nice thing I've ever seen that old man do."

Chapter Twenty-One

Maggie slumped onto the couch and grabbed one of the cookies Elsie deemed too imperfect for the bake sale. *Still tastes amazing.* Brad flopped down next to her, and she leaned her head on his shoulder.

Hollyn sprawled on the other part of the sectional in her Halloween print scrubs with Nixie curled up on her stomach and one arm flung over her face. "Did you have any luck with costumes?"

"No." She reached for another cookie. "All the mall stores are down to the dregs. I refuse to wear anything that has the word 'sexy' in the name."

"Ditto."

Brad snorted. Hollyn groped for a catnip mouse from the carpet and lobbed the toy at him without bothering to open her eyes.

"Maybe we can scrounge scarves and beads to be fortune tellers? That was my fallback when I was a kid."

The front door opened, admitting a breath of crisp fall air and Elsie. She hung up her jacket and bustled over to the couch. "All right you three—sit up and pay attention." She dumped out a couple of shopping bags on the coffee table and rummaged through the contents. She selected a short-sleeved khaki button-down and handed it to Brad. The shirt said "zookeeper" across the back in large block letters.

"Where the heck did you find this?"

"Thrift shops are wonderful places, dear. Just add craft paint."

"I have a ball cap from the zoo I could wear with it."

"Hollyn." She stared at the rumpled lump on the couch until Hollyn sat up properly. Then she passed over a gray sweater spattered with leopard spots that resolved into a cat face. "And these." She added a pair of cat ears on a headband. "Just add some cat's eye eyeliner."

"Some what now?"

"I'll help you," Maggie promised.

Elsie passed her another set of cat ears and a pair of black and purple tiger striped leggings.

"I've got a sparkly purple sweater I can wear with these. Thanks, Elsie." She leaned over and kissed the older woman's cheek.

"Hollyn, do you know what your friend is wearing?"

"Not a clue." She glanced over at Maggie. "He's not likely to turn up in one of those cheesy sexy vampire horrors, is he?"

"Ted? A sexy anything? A giant bag of chips is more likely."

Hollyn stuck her tongue out.

"A donut, maybe?"

****

"Sammy the Safety Dog?" Maggie blinked. Nope. Not a waking nightmare. "You're going to a dance—with a date—and you're wearing the department's safety mascot costume? Have you lost your mind?"

Ted tugged the red vest into place over the tatty black and white spotted fake fur coverall. "I'm a dog. She's a vet. She likes dogs. Besides, you're dressed as a purple cat so it's not like you can talk." He added a red plastic fire helmet with floppy dog ears attached.

No wonder he's single.

"Besides, this afternoon is for kids. How do you know what I'm planning to wear tonight?"

"You? Change clothes?" She shook her head and grabbed a tote full of candy.

"Get a move on, you guys," Kelsey called from the top of the stairs.

****

Brad sipped the cup of hot chocolate Charlie had handed him as he wended his way through throngs of tiny monsters, superheroes, and royalty, each trying to set new records for how much candy they could inhale without their folks noticing. He scanned the impromptu trick or treat stations set up on the sidewalk, looking for Maggie. *There—fire department banner and a goofus in a dalmatian costume. Must be Ted.*

Maggie straightened from having her picture taken with a little witch and grinned at him. The sparkly purple sweater and leggings suited her figure—even better than the fancy dress from last weekend—and the cat's ears gave her a mischievous air that reminded him of Nixie.

"This is amazing. I can't believe the whole thing was pulled together in just a couple of days." She rubbed her hands together, and he offered his cup of chocolate. "Mmm. Thanks."

"Sorry I'm late. I dropped Elsie off at the library for the bake sale, but I had to cruise around to find a parking spot. Looks like the whole town turned out."

She straightened the collar of his zookeeper shirt. "Is Hollyn coming?"

"No, she'll meet us later to get ready for the dance. She has to work. She's teaching Cuthbert how to get around on three legs."

"By herself?"

"Mr. Carson has an appointment. He has to learn, too."

"I heard he made a contribution for the trick or treat. Who knows—maybe he got visited by three ghosts last night."

Brad snorted. "About time." He glanced at Ted, goofing around with a half dozen little kids. "Er…is that what he's wearing to the dance tonight?"

"Heaven only knows." An array of little ghosties and goblins held out their goodie bags with a chorus of trick or treats, and she dropped a sticker in each one.

A toddler in a furry brown costume tugged on the leg of Brad's jeans. "Rowr!"

"What a ferocious little bear cub." He handed the child a packet of cookies and kneeled down so her mother could snap a picture.

The First Ladies bustled over, resplendent in their good witch and bad witch costumes. Mayor Roman touched his arm. "Brad, we have extra ribbons and there's quite a few pets in costume. Would you be willing to judge a pet costume contest?"

"Sure." He glanced at Maggie. "Wanna help?"

"Always." She laced her fingers with his. "Ted?"

He turned, stuffing something chocolate and marshmallow into his mouth.

"Try and save some for the kids, would you? I'm going to help Brad."

He waved her off, still chewing.

They followed the mayor across the green to the gazebo, where the newly crowned Harvest Queen and her court were awarding prizes for kid's costumes. Happy shrieks and screams of trick or treat echoed across the square, along with the occasional not-so-happy squall of a little person who'd had quite enough, thank you very much.

Maggie squeezed his hand. "Are holidays always like this around here?"

He chuckled. "Well, maybe not quite so much sugar, but yeah…we do love our celebrations, and this town is very good at pulling together in a crisis."

The mayor stepped to the microphone. "Thanks everyone for coming today. I know this isn't quite what we were planning, but as always—Carson Mills Cares. Thank you so much for pitching in to make this a safe and happy day for our kids. If anyone needs a break, there's spooky stories all day at the library, and if you're looking for something a little less sugar-laden, Bobbins and Apples has a tent at the end of the green. Now I'd like to invite everyone with a pet in costume to join us here for a contest, judged by our very own Cat Guy."

Pet owners began assembling around the gazebo with their costumed pooches—and one or two cats secured in harnesses. Some pampered pets were part of group costumes with their humans.

"This must have been a wonderful place to grow up. Cupcakes at school and trick or treat in a high rise has nothing on all this."

"See, I was always jealous of kids who got to trick or treat in a big building—so much loot at just one stop."

She squeezed his arm. "Oh my gosh—look at that!" Maggie pointed to a little girl dressed as Red Riding Hood leading a shaggy gray dog on a leash. The dog wore a frilly nightgown and nightcap.

"I dunno. That one's pretty clever." Someone had recycled a plastic e-collar and fashioned a couple of "olives" stuck on a skewer.

"I've heard of sausage dogs, but…a martini dog?"

"Sure looks like it."

Another proud dog owner led three golden labs dressed as the trio of witches from a popular movie.

"How did they ever get them to keep those wigs on?"

"I haven't a clue."

"And how can you pick just one?"

"I guess we better find out how many ribbons there are."

****

"Hold still." Maggie applied teal shadow to Hollyn's eyelids. "And relax your face."

"I don't know why you're bothering. I never wear fancy makeup. You know I'm just gonna forget and rub my eyes and turn myself into a raccoon."

"No, you won't. You're not at work—you're at a party. You won't have any reason to rub your eyes."

"But I have to go back to work after."

Maggie held her breath as she added bold black eyeliner. "Okay. Take a look."

Hollyn blinked in the glaring light of the basement restroom. "Wow. That really is pretty cool."

"Told you." Maggie undid Hollyn's braid and brushed her hair into soft waves.

"What are the guys doing?"

"I think they were corralled into loading supplies or something. At least your brother did. I haven't seen my wayward partner."

A loud rap echoed through the white tiled space. "Hey—you kitty cats, ready to go?"

"Speak of the devil."

191

Hollyn handed her cat's ears to Maggie. "Here, you do it. I'll just make a mess."

"No, you won't." She slid the headband into Hollyn's hair. "There, you look great."

Hollyn peeked in the mirror. "Thanks. Really. I'm no earthly good at girl stuff."

"Come on, Mags!"

She shoved her brush and makeup into a bag. "Hold your horses. I'm sure they won't run out of candy before we get there."

Hollyn opened the door, then stopped dead on the threshold. Maggie bumped into her.

"Ted? Is that you?"

"What? You two never seen a pirate before?" He swept a rakishly feathered hat off his head and bowed over one leg, like something out of a fancy British TV drama.

"Are you some sort of cartoon character?" Hollyn peered at him owlishly.

"Hey—this took me a few years to put together. This stuff ain't cheap you know." He straightened the ruffled cuffs of his shirt more fastidiously than she'd ever seen him treat his day to day clothes.

Maggie heaved a sigh. "Did you bother to look in a mirror while you were changing, Captain Candy?" She dragged him into the ladies room and faced him toward a mirror.

The black nose and whiskers he'd drawn on his face earlier stared back, slightly smeared.

She rummaged through her bag for a pack of wipes. "Here."

He took one and rubbed ineffectually at his face. "Got anything stronger?"

"Those are professional-grade makeup wipes." She grabbed his chin and scrubbed briskly with a fresh wipe. "What is this?"

"It said it washed off with soap and water, so I just washed up in the sink and figured it was gone."

"But what is it? Kid's Halloween makeup from the drugstore?"

"Um…washable marker."

"And you put it on your face?"

He shrugged.

"You know I had eyeliner, right?"

"There's a difference?"

Hollyn pawed through her own bag. "Here. These are antibacterial. The alcohol should shift that ink."

Maggie rolled her eyes and kept scrubbing.

"Leave some skin, willya?"

"Next time, ask for help. There were plenty of moms around. One of them must have had something better than magic marker."

"Is the ink coming off?"

Hollyn tilted her head, studying his face. "The marker's faded a lot. I think with the fancy lighting in the gym, it'll just look like soot or something. That works, right?"

"Soot from musket fire—perfect."

"That's a really great outfit. It looks like something from a movie."

"Renaissance faire, actually." He straightened and adjusted the red silk scarf wrapped around his waist.

Maggie gathered the used wipes from the sink. "I didn't know you were into that."

"There's a lot you don't know about me."

"Who are you and what have you done with my

partner?"

He ignored her and offered Hollyn his arm.

She straightened her sweater and linked her arm through his. "I've always wanted to visit one of those fairs."

"You'd love it. The food is amazing. Steak on a stake, giant turkey legs, fried mac and cheese—"

"How do you fry mac and cheese?"

"Maybe you could come with me some time and find out?"

****

Brad was waiting for her outside by the car. The square was mostly deserted now, families heading home to deal with the monumental sugar crash. Mitch and his gang had broken down their tent and retreated to the diner, leaving a faint ghost of salty-sweet kettle corn trailing on the breeze.

She shivered and shrugged into her jacket. Purple and orange lights from store windows threw spooky shadows on the sidewalk and jack-o-lanterns cast a flickering glow over the steps. Skeletons of deserted candy stations waited for the morning cleanup crews. A few stray candy wrappers and coffee cups skittered along the gutter, but nowhere near the mess she'd expect from such a crowd. Brad straightened and grinned when he saw her. "I was afraid I was gonna have to call your buddies from Search and Rescue."

Maggie chuckled. "Some of us take longer to get ready for a party than others."

"What, you mean Hollyn?"

"No. Not exactly." She glanced over her shoulder.

He blinked at the swashbuckling apparition. "Is that…Ted?"

"Apparently so." She took his hand. "Now, don't go all big brother, but they're discussing a trip to the renaissance faire next summer."

"Well, like everyone keeps telling me, she's a grown woman. She's allowed to socialize with anyone she wants."

"Even a guy who thinks washable marker is a good substitute for makeup?"

"Do I want to know?"

"Probably not."

He took her other hand, rubbing his thumbs over her knuckles. His grip was warm, steady, and dependable. *Just like him.* She shivered at the gentle contact.

"So, what happens next? I saw checklists for Thanksgiving and Christmas already posted in town hall."

He chuckled softly. "Well, tomorrow we'll clean all this up, and transform everything to Thanksgiving— really Thanksgiving, no Christmas stuff until the day after."

"I like the sound of that."

"Are you…that is, do you have family to go to for the holidays?"

She shook her head. "Not anymore."

"Well, you do now."

"I really like the sound of that."

"Wait till you taste Elsie's turkey. Look, before we get into the clown car with those two, or worse, the gym full of sugar-crazed preteens, I just wanted to say—you look beautiful."

Her cheeks warmed. "You've been looking at me all afternoon. All I did was brush my hair and touch up my makeup."

He tightened his grip on her hands. "You look beautiful crawling through the woods helping me trap kittens or up in the middle of the night feeding bottle babies. I should probably tell you more often."

She sidled a bit closer. "You're not so bad yourself, you know." She freed one hand and brushed her fingers through his hair.

He kissed the hand he held and wrapped both his own around it. "I'm so glad I met you."

"So am I."

He leaned down and kissed her, softly, gently—the way he handled the fragile little lives in his care. She slid her arm around his neck, deepening the kiss. He cradled her cheek in one hand and wrapped his other arm around her waist.

"Break it up you two," Ted called cheerfully. "We're supposed to be chaperoning kids, not volunteers."

They broke apart ever so slightly. Brad rested his forehead on hers, trying to catch his breath. "Do we really have to go to this thing?"

"We promised."

"With them?"

" 'Fraid so."

"But maybe after?"

Her lips curved in a mischievous smile. "Definitely after."

"Happy Halloween, Maggie." He matched her smile with one of his own, then leaned in and kissed her again.

Author's Note

In case you're wondering, people like Brad, Hollyn, and Elsie really exist. They have an enormous impact on the lives of the individual cats and kittens that they rescue. They also help educate the public about the benefits of spaying and neutering pets. Just search for kitten rescues on your favorite social media platform to see their incredible work. (And, of course, laugh at the antics of adorable silly kittens.)

Thank you for purchasing
this publication of The Wild Rose Press, Inc.

For questions or more information
contact us at
info@thewildrosepress.com.

The Wild Rose Press, Inc.
www.thewildrosepress.com